Say My Name Boy

T. Brian Loos

Published by T. Brian Loos, 2023.

Say My Name Boy

By T.Brian Loos

Published by T.Brian Loos

© 2018 T.Brian Loos

SAY MY NAME BOY

First edition. June 24, 2023.

Copyright © 2023 T. Brian Loos.

ISBN: 979-8223237037

Written by T. Brian Loos.

On Father's day 2015 I was 25 years old. I never had a girlfriend and my parents kept asking me if I don't wanna start dating soon. They had the daughter of Dad's coworker Colton in mind. She was a nice girl and my parents liked her alot. But I was always more interested in guys. I remember checking out guys, when I was still in kindergarten.

Father's day was on a Saturday, Mom visited her Dad over the weekend. Dad and I stayed at home and were planning on having a BBQ with Dad's friend Colton and his daughter. Dad marinated the meat in the kitchen and prepared everything for the cookout. In the meantime I decided to take a shower. "Hey Dad, I'm taking a shower and jack off, don't walk in on me, ok ? I'm so fucking horny," I shouted at Dad downstairs. "Ok, take your time and enjoy. I guess you didn't find a pussy to fuck, huh ? Colton and his daughter should be here any minute and we don't want them to see you walking around with a boner," he said and laughed. I never met Colton or his daughter, I only heard my parents talking about them. Colton was divorced and raised his 20 year old daughter Mercedes as a single parent.

I went to the bathroom, threw my boxers on the floor and jumped in the shower. I soaped up and rinsed off. I opened the shower curtain, pulled my foreskin back and put a generous amount of body wash on my cock. I layed down on the bathroom floor and started to stroke my hard cock. My dick was covered in foam and I was close to shooting my nut on the floor, when suddenly the door was opened by an incredibly handsome, sexy looking man in his late thirties. The upper half of his shirt was unbuttoned and I could see his hairy chest. He had a five o'clock beard and a few tattoos on both of his arms. And here I was laying naked on the bathroom floor and stroking my cock in front of this sexy stranger. I was so embarrassed and felt my face blushing. But at the same time it turned me on and I could feel my seed rising up my pulsating fuck pole. Two more strokes and my nut juice sprayed out of my cock and landed on the floor right in front of the guy.

"Hi, I'm Colton. Thanks for welcoming me in this hot way, I can tell it came from the bottom of your nuts," he said and smiled. "I just wanted to take a piss if you don't mind," Colton said. I couldn't say anything, I just watched him pulling his dark tanned, veiny cock out of his pants and holding it over the toilet. A strong stream of his man piss sprayed into the water in the toilet and made a loud splashing sound. He noticed my cock getting hard again.

"Aw, you're one of them fucking faggot boys who love the taste of Nature's Champagne, huh ? Get in the tub you little fucker, I show you something. Nah, never mind, it's too late. I already pissed it all out." He shaked his dick off and pushed it back in his pants. "See ya outside boy, your Dad just heated up the grill," he said and left the bathroom. The big bulge in his pants looked like he stuffed a few socks in there but I had proof enough, he didn't need anything stuffed down his pants. I dried off and put my shorts on. It was warm enough to be without a t-shirt. I went downstairs and saw Dad and Colton sitting on the couch in the living room. They both didn't wear a shirt and were sitting there only in their boxers. "Hey son, this is my friend and coworker Colton, Colton this is my son Kent. We got a little more comfortable since we have the house to ourselves, that's why we are sitting around in boxers," my Dad explained.

He got up and went outside in the backyard. We had a privacy fence around the property so we could be naked in our yard if we wanted to.

"Don't worry you horny little fucker," Colton almost whispered,"there is enough beer in the fridge to fill you up with my piss." I heard about guys pissing on each other but I never tried it and it didn't really sound hot or exciting to me. But I'm always up to try everything at least once. On the other hand, this sexy stud Colton could do anything to me. Just thinking about him and his deep manly voice made my cock and fuckhole twitch. He was still sitting on the couch. "Speaking about beer, do you want one ? I get one for myself anyway," I asked Colton. "Sure, I'll take one."

When I walked by Colton to get the beers, I had to check out his crotch. His cock and balls made the boxers bulge out between his legs. I saw the tip of his cock head and one nut hanging out on his left leg. His piss slit was glistening with precum. He looked at me and blinked with his right eye. I took two beers out of the fridge, when Dad came back inside. "I take one too son. You know," he said to Colton, "if you want, you and Mercedes can always stay overnight and take the guest bedroom. That way you don't have to drive home after drinking beer." Colton agreed and took the beer I gave him, brushing his hand against mine. Dad took his beer and went back outside to entertain Mercedes, since I was more interested in her Dad. Colton saw my dick stiffening in my shorts after I saw his breeding tool hanging out. I wanted him so bad right then and there and he must've read my mind.

"Hey you little brat, can you show me the guest room so I can get settled in ? I may take a shower myself. Your Dad and my daughter should be busy with the BBQ for a while," he said to me. I was so excited in anticipation of what may happen, my knees were shaky. He took his clothes from the couch and followed me upstairs to the guest room. He put his clothes and a small overnight bag on the bed. It seemed like he came prepared and knew he would stay over night. "Wanna soap up my back," he asked me. I nodded and followed him into the bathroom like a little pup. He pulled his boxers down and was standing naked in front of me. He opened my fly and the button of my shorts so they could slipp down to the floor. Our cocks got hard at the same time and we stepped into the shower. He grabbed my dick with his right hand and pulled my foreskin all the way back, while he fingered my asshole with his left middle finger. I didn't even soap up his back yet. He took a bar soap and slid it up and down my ass crack until my hole was covered with foam. Colton grabbed me by my hips and lined his cock head up with my fuckhole. I never got fucked before,

Colton's cock was the first one that penetrated me. He pushed and forced his hard rod inside my fucktube. I whimpered for a few seconds but the thought of having this hot sexy man's cock inside of me, turned the pain into pure excessive lust and pleasure. I felt his piston going back and forth inside of me and Colton started moaning. I backed up against his crotch to have his cock as deep as possible inside of me. "Yeah you horny little fucker, take my seed. I'm gonna inseminate you and I want you to keep my semen inside of you until your body absorbs it completely. Then you will be a part of me." His cock started to jerk and he was moaning even more, when I felt his cum spraying inside of me. Colton didn't pull his cock out of my fuckhole when he was done inseminating me. His cum wasn't the only thing he wanted to give me, he also pissed in my ass.

It felt warm and I loved the feeling, when his cum and piss got mixed up. He pulled out carefully so nothing would leak out of me. He sneaked out of the bathroom naked to get a butt plug from his room. "Here boy, open up wide. It's a big one but it makes it easier for you to keep my man juices inside." He put the plug on my hole and with one swift push Colton inserted that monster plug and stretched my fuck muscle to the max. He made me whimper once again but I loved it and thanked him. "I will walk funny with all that stuff in me, don't you think Colton ?"

"Yeah, I would love to see that, but you better lay down on the bed for 15 minutes," Colton said and laughed. He went downstairs to my Dad and his daughter.

After about 20 minutes I jumped into the shower again and pulled the plug. Coltons piss was gushing out of my ass and splashed down on the shower bottom. I went down on my knees, hoping to see some of Colton's cum in his piss. I saw something that looked like stringy snot, floating in his musky smelling piss.

I rinsed my ass off, put my shorts on and went outside to Dad, Colton and his daughter. Mercedes looked at me and started to laugh.

Since I didn't have a boner, I was very confident it wasn't me she was laughing about.

"Hey Kent, this is my daughter Mercedes. I don't think you both met before," Colton said.

"Hi Kent, nice to meet you finally. How's it going? I heard quite a bit about you. Oh, by the way, you have a wet spot right there, where your ass hole is. That's why I laughed," and she pointed at my ass.

How could she embarrass me like that, right in front of everybody.

"Is she always that straight out and outspoken," I asked Colton. He laughed and answered: "Yeah unfortunately she is, but don't worry, she usually likes you when she does it."

"Well, that's a lovely way to show it," I said.

"I'm sorry if I embarrassed you, I always talk before I think. But anyway, you're a good looking guy, we should go out on a date some time. Come over here, you can sit next to me if you want. You're not gay, are you ? If you are, you can tell me. That would explain the wet spot on your ass," and she laughed again.

I already hated her and it seemed like she never shuts up. But not to be rude, I was sitting next to her. I would rather sit next to her Dad but she ruined it. How could a smart, sexy and handsome man like Colton produce such an obnoxious human creature, I was thinking to myself. She probably got it from her mother, no wonder Colton divorced her.

Dad took the meat off the grill and put it on the table. "So kids, you both should really go out together. You would make a nice couple," my Dad said.

"Dad, please. We just met. You're gonna make her blush if you talk like that," I said to Dad.

"Nah, that's ok. I don't blush very easily," she responded. We all grabbed some meat with baked beans and began to eat. I looked over to Colton and saw him glancing over to me too. We were almost done eating, when I felt a hand on my right leg, sliding up closer to my crotch. I didn't know what to do or what to say. Mercedes's left hand was the only one that wasn't on the table. Her hand actually touched my dick through the shorts. She massaged, pinched and rubbed on it, trying to get me hard.

Needless to say, she was out of luck. I jumped up and said: "I have to go to the bathroom. I'm right back." I went inside the house and sat down on the couch to wait a few minutes to make them think I had to piss. I thought when I went back outside, I would sit down next to Colton. Someone opened the back door. I was hoping Colton followed me but I heard her voice calling me.

"Kent, it's me. You wanna go to your room ? You don't wanna do it down here on the couch, do you ? Did I turn you on ? I figured you would be horny and hard for me in a heartbeat. Your dick really feels like it's a fat one."

"What ? Listen, I'm gay. I never touched a woman and I'm not planning on doing it. But don't tell my Dad please," I said to her. I felt better and released after telling her.

"Aw, ok. Why didn't you tell me right away? I'm fine with that. Daddy fucks guys in the ass all the time. You should stop by later or tomorrow, he probably fucks you too if you want. Do you like him," she asked.

"Liking him ? I adore him," I said and told her about how her Dad fucked me earlier. I figured I could use her to my advantage and ask a few questions about her Dad to get to know him as much as possible .

"Wow, look at us, we're chatting away like two best friends," I said. We talked for about 15 minutes at least before we went back outside.

"Hey, welcome back you two, I bet you both had a good time inside," my Dad said with a smile.

"Well I'm glad you both got to know each other and get along well. This way you don't have to worry about stopping by our house if you want Kent. If Mercedes doesn't like someone, she lets them clearly know," Colton said.

"I'm sure she does," I answered.

Mercedes got picked up by a friend shortly after dinner. Colton, Dad and I had a few more beers after she left. Dad and Colton talked about work for most of the evening. Colton noticed that I was bored and tried to change the subject. But Dad interrupted him and asked me: "So son, what did you both do in here ? Did you fuck her or what ? It would have been better if you hadn't jerked off earlier today."

"Oh Dad, stop it. Believe me, I didn't regret it at all, that I polished my meat and got off. "I wouldn't mind doing it again." I looked at Colton and smiled.

Around eleven o'clock Dad went into his bedroom and Colton in the guest room. I closed the door to my room about ten minutes later.

Around midnight I woke up from some noises coming from Dad's room that sounded like moaning and a squeaking bed. I thought Dad was stroking off to porn. I turned around and fell asleep again.

It was already daylight when I woke up but still early. I looked at my alarm clock. 6.10am. My dick was hard and I needed to stroke off again. I pulled my foreskin back and put some lube on the head before I began to stroke, pulling the skin back and forth over my cock head. The lube under my foreskin made that typical sloshing jerk off sound. I was thinking about Colton and how he fucked me in the bathroom the day before. I was wondering if he was already awake. Probably horny himself and laying on his bed with a boner. I got up and sneaked out of my room, still naked with a hard on. I tiptoed to Colton's door and listened for any sound coming from his room.

But it was quiet. I slowly turned the doorknob and carefully pushed the door open. My heart was racing for excitement. I imagined Colton sleeping naked on his bed, his pulsating hard cock standing straight up his belly and leaking precum. I would sneak over to his bed and lick the cum droplets off his tip. He would wake up, grab me by my hips and fuck the shit out of me.

But the bed was empty. His bag and clothes were gone. What happened last night ? Did I miss something ?

I layed down on Colton's bed and smelled his scent on the bed sheets. I could smell a light musky scent where his dick and balls were laying on the sheet. I took a deep breath and closed my eyes. I imagined his cock was still there. I kept stroking my cock and only a few seconds later my cum sprayed all over the bed sheets. I was in a daze when I orgasmed and I heard myself saying Colton's name over and over again and Colton I love you. I was hoping Dad didn't hear me. I went back to my room and put my boxers on before I went to the bathroom to take my morning piss and flush the cum residue out of my pipe.

I was kinda disappointed that Colton didn't stay all night. I would've loved to have breakfast with him. I went downstairs to the kitchen, where I heard some noises coming from. It smelled like freshly brewed coffee and I thought maybe Colton was in the kitchen making breakfast. My heart started beating faster again. I stepped into the kitchen but there was no Colton. "Mom ! What are you doing here so early ? Didn't you wanna stay at grandpa's until this afternoon ?" I asked her.

"Good morning to you too son. Yes I was gonna stay there until later today. But I decided to come back home sooner. I got a little nervous and worried, when your Dad didn't pick up the phone last night. Usually he is still up around midnight," Mom answered.

"Actually he went to bed at elevenish last night. Why would you be worried," I asked her.

"Well you never know about him. He's a dog, he fucks everything that has a hole."

"Everything ?" I asked her.

"You know what I mean. He had probably every blond Bimbo in this town. Are you sure Dad was in bed ? You didn't notice or hear anything," Mom asked.

"No, not really," I said.

It seemed like Mom didn't know about Colton staying overnight and Colton left before she came back home. Was what I heard in Dad's room not Dad just jacking off to porn ? But I didn't hear any woman coming into the house last night. On the other hand I was sleeping and didn't hear anything.

When Dad came downstairs, we had breakfast together. Nobody talked much that morning. It seemed like everyone was busy with their own thoughts. Around 10 am Dad's phone was ringing. Dad picked up and I heard a female voice on the other end. "Oh,hi Mercedes. Yes Kent is here, hold on a second. Kent ! Mercedes wants to ask you something," I heard Dad saying. What did she want from me. I told her I was gay. I took the phone and said: "Hello, what's up ?"

"Hey Kent, it's Mercedes."

"I know, what's up ?"

"Well, I wanted to ask you if you wanna come over today and watch a movie or so. I have to leave soon though but my Dad is home and probably could need some help around here."

It took me a while until I got her drift. "Oh yeah, yes of course I come over and watch a movie with you. Give me a few," I said to her and hung up. I was sure Mom and Dad were happy when I was going to chill with Mercedes. "Mom ! Mom, I go and watch a movie with Mercedes. We stayed at her house."

"Oh, that's a great idea. Did you finally hook up with her? I told you she's a Sweetheart," Mom answered.

"Yeah you were right Mom, she is great."

I got more nervous the closer I got to Colton's house. I didn't wanna do or say anything stupid. I wanted to impress him as much as possible. I was proud about the fact, that this stud wanted to hang and fuck around with me. It strengthened my self esteem and I wanted everybody of my friends to know about me and him, but it wasn't possible.

I entered through the big wrought iron gate and drove up a little hill to the house. Mercedes was already gone to my relief. Her car wasn't there. The house was built in the style of a castle and had a shiny copper roof. It was situated on at least 20 acres of well maintained park like land. My heart was pounding faster again and my testosterone level must have been to the max.

Colton saw me coming and opened the door.

"Hey baby boy, how's it hanging," he greeted me and brushed his hand against my cock.

"It's hanging just fine but not for much longer, that's for sure," I joked. We went outside to the porch and had a drink. "So are we alone or is somebody else here ? This place is huge," I asked Colton.

"No, we're alone. Let's get naked and jump in the pool."

"Oh yeah, and then have sex in the pool house," I said.

"Sounds good to me, the pool house it is. But just for future reference, a castle always comes with a dungeon. So if you up for wild kinky sex in a dungeon or for making love in my bedroom, let me know," Colton said.

I would definitely give my right arm to make love to Colton but a five minute fuck is hot too. I didn't know what he meant by a castle comes with a dungeon though, but I'm sure I will find out sooner or later.

We threw our clothes on the grass and jumped into the pool. There was a waterfall in front of a small man-made cave, just big enough for about five people. In the center of the pool was an island with two lawn chairs and a table. The island was connected to the pool deck through a small bridge. I could've spent all day out there by the pool.

"Hey Colton," I said," how did you get a property like this ?" I just had to ask. If he is really my Dad's coworker he wouldn't make enough money to afford a place like this.

"I figured you would ask. First of all I'm not working with your Dad. We just made that up so your Mom and other people wouldn't ask how we met. I inherited this property from my father about 18 years ago when he died at the age of 92 years.

He was a very, very wealthy man. I can live extremely comfortably and don't have to work for the rest of my life," Colton explained.

"Wow," was all I could say at that moment.

But how did he and my Dad meet ? I asked Colton about it later the same day. I didn't wanna ask too many questions about him at once, so he wouldn't think I'm a nosy drama queen.

He told me he met my Dad at one of his dungeon group sex parties. That also explained my question about the dungeon. I was shocked. My Dad had sex with Colton and other guys in a dungeon. A feeling of jealousy was stuck in my chest from that moment on. Just the thought of Colton having sex with someone else drove me crazy. But I didn't want him to notice or know how I felt about him. At least not at that moment. After all, for Colton I was just a fuck buddy who met him only once before. I hoped that would change.

"Hey Kent, still wanna do the pool house fuck ?"

"Hell yeah, but if you'd rather go to your bedroom I don't mind," I told him.

"Yes, I think I'm in the mood to make love to you in my bedroom," Colton said.

We dried off in the sun for a few minutes before we went inside the house. I was a bit confused, if he wants to make love to me, does that mean I'm more than just a fuck buddy ?

I entered the bedroom first, my dick left a trail of cock snot throughout the house, leading to the bedroom. I always leaked precum more than other guys.

We laid down on Colton's bed

and he kissed me on the lips.

I raised my butt up and pulled my ass cheeks apart. Coltons cock didn't stay soft for much longer. He wanted to penetrate me laying on our sides, so I had to change position. He snuggled up from behind me, holding me in his arms, kissing my neck, sniffing and licking my armpits. I felt his hard cock pushing against my tight, still closed fuckhole. The tip was wet from his precum and worked great as lube on my hole. He pushed harder, slowly pushing his head through my hole. He felt the resistance of my ass muscle subsiding, as his head popped completely through my sphincter. I took a deep breath and enjoyed every millimeter of Colton's penis. I could feel his cock massaging my prostate, squeezing even more precum out of my dick. He made me produce my own lube I used to stroke my cock. Colton pumped his cock faster and more forcefully into my ass, started to sweat and breathe harder. He was whispering in my ear, he is gonna inseminate me with all his seed and love he has for me. I could smell his sweaty armpits and the sweet musky smell of his hairy crotch. His ecstatic man scent made me feel like melting wax being shaped by his hard pounding cock. It felt like Colton and I were one entity. Sex never felt as great before as with Colton.

He bucked his hips, his cock began to jerk and I felt his seed filling up my love tunnel.

He was the first man who made me cum just by pounding my ass. I shot my load only a few seconds after he did. I was so overwhelmed by feelings of lust and love, I had tears in my eyes when I sprayed my cum on his hand.When he saw my tears, he licked them off my cheeks, then he licked my cum off his hand.

"Colton, this was the best sex I ever had. Thank you for coming into my life."

"Same here baby boy, same here. It was amazing," he said.

"Are you still hosting your dungeon parties ? I'm kinda curious about it. I have never joined or seen something like that. I would be too nervous anyway to do anything but you and I could play together while the other guys do their thing," I asked Colton.

"The last time I hosted a party was about three month ago. But if you want, we can set up one for Independence day."

"Ok, cool. Can I ask you a favor ? Can we invite my Dad too ? But don't tell him I'm here. I have an idea that will be very helpful in the near future," I asked Colton.

"Sure, why not. I'm gonna invite him. But don't you think it will be awkward for you with your Dad being naked and having sex right in front of you ?"

"Yeah for him, not for me. That's part of the plan," I said to Colton.

"Alright then baby boy."

We went back outside to the pool for a while before I had to head back home. It was getting late and I had to be at work the next morning.

"Have a safe trip home. You wanna come over again tomorrow ?" Colton asked me.

"Sure, I wish I wouldn't have to work, I could stay overnight. I can imagine the pool by night must be gorgeous," I answered him.

It was about a one hour drive from my house to Colton. I wished it was closer. By 11 pm I arrived at home. I sent Colton a short text that I made it home safely.

The next morning I got ready for work, got in my car and it didn't start.

I called a tow truck and had it towed to my mechanic. "Fuel pump," he said. "Takes about five days to fix." Just what I needed I was thinking to myself. I called Colton and told him about my car and that I couldn't come over. I didn't hear from him until two days later, when he called and told me he was missing me and asked if he could come over to my parents house. Of course I said yes and I was happy he thought about me and missed me. Ninety minutes later I saw him pulling in the driveway. Dad had a night shift that week so he was home. "Daaad ! Your coworker is here," I yelled through the house.

"What is he doing here, he didn't say he's coming over." my Dad said and went to the door to let Colton in.

"Hey man what's up," Dad said. Mom was in the kitchen and came into the living room when she heard Colton talking. "Oh hi Colton," she said, "where is your lovely daughter ? Why didn't you take her with you so Kent had some company too."

Here we go again, I thought to myself. We were all sitting in the living room and small talked about bullshit stuff. I wished my parents would go somewhere so Colton and I had some alone time. But they didn't.

Colton and I made the best out of it and acted like we hardly knew each other. It was kinda fun.

"Kent was your name if I remember right, wasn't it," Colton said, "don't you wanna get your own place instead of living with your parents ? You should come over to my place some day and use the pool if you want. And you can hang out with Mercedes again. You both had such a great time last Sunday."

Mom of course liked that idea.

"Yes that sounds cool but right now my car is in the shop," I said to him.

He stayed for about one hour before he had to leave.

"Well nice seeing you again Kent," Colton said and shaked my Moms and Dads hand.

"Yep, same here, it was nice seeing ya," I said.

The next two days until my car was done we talked a few times on the phone. Nothing special, just to say hi and stay in touch.

Finally it was Saturday and I could pick up my car. From the shop I went straight to Colton's house.

"Hey baby boy, come in," he said when he opened the door for me. "Well obviously you survived one week without having sex, or did you fuck somebody," I asked Colton.

"No I didn't fuck anybody, I was thinking about it though. But it was weird, when I was about to hook up, I was feeling bad. That never happened before. And what about you ?"

"I had wild and passionate sex with my right hand," I told Colton.

"Well let's make up for it today baby boy," he said.

I had to take a piss and went to the bathroom. I found Colton's underwear on the floor. He probably forgot to pick it up after he showered. I took it off the floor and was holding it close to my face. I sniffed the area where Colton's ass was, then where his nuts and dick were hanging. The light sweet musky scent made my cock rock hard. I forgot all about pissing. After a while Colton was wondering where I was and checked on me in the bathroom. He had to piss himself anyway so we both stood next to each other at the toilet and let our piss flow into the toilet bowl. Colton was first who moved his cock to the side and pissed on my cock. I did the same and pissed on his big veiny cock. It made him hard instantly.

"Let's role play," he said. "You're the bad, bad houseboy and I just caught you in the laundry room stealing my used underwear and jerking off on it. I fuck you right there on the washer as your punishment."

"Punishment, yeah right," I said and had to laugh. Sounds hot, come on and punish your houseboy in the laundry room," I said. We walked down the stairs to the basement, where the laundry room was. I got naked and jumped on the washer, my legs up in the air, giving Colton easy access to my cock milking hole. Colton slammed his rigid boner with one hard push into my waiting hole. I took him like a man. It didn't even hurt much that time. I could tell, he didn't have sex during the past five days. He really was faithful to me. His fuck rod slid in and out of me, generating the needed friction to make his seed boil in his nuts. He spit on his hand and polished my dick head until we both were close to climax. Colton screamed and stopped thrusting his hips, his ball sack stopped slapping against my ass and he ejaculated his semen deep into my bowels. "I didn't get off yet babe," I said to him and took over polishing my head. But I stopped before I drained my nut juice on my belly. I had an idea.

I jumped off the washer and stood in front of Colton. I grabbed our cocks, pulled my foreskin back and pressed our dick heads together. Then I pulled my skin over mine and his head and started stroking with a tight grip. Colton moaned and got hard again. The sight of his cock head being covered by my foreskin turned him on. I shot my load with forceful pressure underneath my skin.Colton couldn't resist the tight milking of my hand and added his white gold, mixing his seed with mine underneath my foreskin. When we both were spent, I pulled my skin slowly back and our cum splashed down on the tile floor. "Wow that was hot," Colton said and scooped our cum off the floor and licked it off his finger. The tip of his dick head still had some cum drops on it. I took his head between my fingers and licked every drop off it. He told me to stop touching his over sensitized head but I kept licking and rubbing it until he couldn't stand it anymore and pulled his breeder away from my hands. I couldn't get enough from this man. I spread his ass cheeks instead and put my nose between them, inhaling the manly smell of his hole.

"Damn you are an evil boy, aren't you," he said.

"Who is evil," said a voice coming from the door. We both panicked for a few seconds and tried to put our shorts back on as fast as possible. Mercedes was back home and heard us in the basement.

"Well I guess I missed the interesting part," she said and laughed.

"Go back upstairs and don't spy on innocent gay men having a blast," Colton told his daughter. "Yeah yeah I'm going."

She seemed disappointed when she turned around and left.

"You should air out the room, it smells like cum and ass in there," she shouted back at us.

"Whatever. You're just jealous because your Dad gets more cock than you do," Colton yelled at her.

We went outside to the pool and jumped in the water.

"Do you wanna stay tonight ? Mercedes should be gone soon,usually I don't see her all weekend," Colton asked me.

"Hell yeah, sure shit." I finally got to spend my first night together with Colton. I even put up with his daughter for that.

We went out for dinner to a gay restaurant. It was the first time I was out in public with Colton. I noticed a lot of guys were checking him out. But he was there with me and it boosted my self esteem. I wanted everybody to think that he is my boyfriend. It made me feel good.

"So is this our first date," I asked him.

"Actually yes, it is. I didn't even think about it. Let's call it our first dinner date. God knows we already had a few fuck dates. And Mercedes knows too since today," he added and laughed.

Three guys were sitting at a table across from us, one of them didn't stop stirring at Colton or I should say his crotch. They already paid and were about to leave. They got up and two of them walked towards the door but the third one stood just there and kept stirring. He had a piece of paper in his hand. He came over to our table and gave it to Colton with a smile. He actually wrote his phone number and "Call me" on it. Colton took the note and asked the guy friendly: "Why would you think I wanna call you ? Don't you see I'm here with somebody ?"

But the guy was even bolder than I thought. He said: "Yes I can see you're here with somebody. But can't you see he is no boyfriend material ? He is too young for you. It's your decision but your loss if you don't call me."

I jumped off my chair and was about to punch him in his face. Colton caught my fist at the last second and calmed me down.

"Don't get your hands dirty on this guy babe, he's not worth it."

That was the first time he called me babe, except the few times when he called me baby boy.

Then he looked at the guy, ripped the paper in hundred pieces, threw them in front of his feet and said: "Well, for your information, we only fuck dogs. They have probably bigger dicks than what you have hanging between your legs. And looking at your face, it seems like your Dad fucked a rat."

I couldn't believe what Colton just said. And the guy even believed the dog story. He turned red in his face from anger or embarrassment, I don't know, but he left in a hurry. I was laughing my ass off after the guy was gone and Colton said: "We should've invited him to our next dungeon party and humiliated him in front of everybody. He thinks he is God's gift."

We were ready to go home and relax on the couch or at the pool. I called my parents to let them know I'm staying overnight at Colton's house with Mercedes. I couldn't tell them about me being gay and fuck around with my Dad's coworker. Not yet.

When we got home, we skipped the couch and went straight to bed. Colton turned on the tv in the bedroom and I snuggled up to him. He put his arm around me and pulled me close to his chest. I smelled his armpit and I put my nose closer to it so I wouldn't waste any of Colton's homemade aphrodisiac.

"Are you horny again you little fucker," he asked me.

"I'm getting there, a few more whiffs of your pit sweat and I'm ready to roll."

"I had a great day today.Wouldn't it be nice if we could always be together ? You wouldn't have to work either, I told you I got enough money. If you want, you can move in with me any time. Tell your parents you're renting a room for me to be closer to Mercedes."

"That's a friggin fuck'n good idea. I can get my stuff tomorrow if that's ok with you," I told Colton.

"Yep, sure. I'm glad you like the idea," he said.

The next day I picked up my stuff from my parents house. My Mom thought it's too soon to move into the same house with Mercedes but she didn't really mind. She liked her too much to say anything negative about it.

"Dad, have you ever been over at Colton's house ? You should visit some time," I asked my Dad and played dumb.

"No, I have never been there. I heard it is a big property though," he said.

"I have to head back, Mercedes is probably worried about me," I said and left.

Unfortunately Mercedes was home when I arrived there. Her Dad already told her about me moving in with him.

"Hey, do I have to call you stepdad now ? You guys getting married ? Well anyway, I'm happy for you guys. I guess you gonna get fucked daily now. Lucky you. I saw my Dads dick one time and I can totally understand your excitement," Mercedes said and grinned.

"But I also have good news. I found myself a guy with a huge cock and he fucks me silly all day long. I will move in with him next week," she said.

"I'm glad to hear that. But I really don't need to know what you guys are doing all day, I really don't want to know," I said to her.

I brought all my stuff to the bedroom and got settled in.

I didn't quit my job right away, I wanted to wait and see how things were going between Colton and me.

The days went by in a breeze and we both were glad we made the decision to move in together. The invitations for the Independence day dungeon party were all sent out. Colton invited my Dad by phone rather than sending him an invitation by mail. That way Mom couldn't find any evidence. He told him I didn't know about the dungeon party, and that I live in the east wing of the house with Mercedes. I wouldn't even see any of the guests or activities. Dad was fine with that.

Finally Independence day was there. The guests were supposed to show up at 11 pm. The dungeon was clean and equipped with lube, condoms and refreshments. I was a bit nervous about the party. It was my first time ever I attended a sex party.

It was eleven o'clock sharp, when the first guys showed up. My Dad was one of them. I never knew he was such a horny dog. Before everybody could enter the dungeon, they had to strip their clothes off at the door. Colton and I were already naked and he greeted everyone at the door. I was still hiding in a dark corner of the room. The moment I was waiting for, was so close. And there was Dad. He came into the room with four other guys. The dungeon filled quickly. Ten minutes after eleven everybody of the twenty invited men was there. I saw my Dad for the first time naked. He was also uncut like I was but his dick was about an inch longer than mine. He was already hard and sucking on a few cocks. A guy with even a few more inches than Dad, stepped behind him and pulled Dad's ass cheeks apart. Before I realized it, Dad got fucked. That big cock stuck in his ass and worked its way down to the base of that massive shaft. I walked over to them and called: "Daaad !" When he heard my voice his body froze and he lost his boner. "Dad, I'm sorry I have to interrupt you and I really hope your dick gets hard again but I need to talk to you."

"Son, ah Kent, what are you doing here ?"

"The same as you Dad, well not exactly the same, I don't cheat on my partner as you do. But see that's where my deal comes in. I won't tell Mom if you keep your paws off Colton, he won't bother you either because we are a couple and probably getting married. You tell Mom I'm gay and you're fine with it. You make her accepting me being gay. That's all I want."

It was too much info at once for Dad, he had to sit down. But the guy was still fucking Dad in the ass.

"Ok no problem. I do what you want if you don't tell your Mom," Dad said.

"Great, then we have a deal. Now have fun and enjoy yourself as I do too," I said to Dad and went back to the other side of the room where Colton was watching two guys fisting.

"Hey babe what do you wanna do ? Tell me your most perverted fantasy," I asked Colton.

"We should try a sounding experiment tonight, you want to ?"

"Fuck yeah." I said. He walked over to the toy box and took a hollow steel rod. Colton and I were standing in the center of the room, facing each other. His cock was already hard. I grabbed his nuts, holding and slightly squeezing them. He inserted one end of the steel sound into his piss slit and pushed it down his urethra until half of the rod disappeared inside his shaft. The other end he pushed down my cock and when I had about half of the sound inside my dick, his and my dick head were touching each other. Our cocks were impaled by a hollow steel rod. It was hot to look at. One guy said: "I need to take a pic of Colton's and Kent's cock fucking each other from the inside." A cute little guy was standing right next to us. He was bending over, spreading his ass cheeks and showed us both his pink fuckhole. He was a cute little pup with some silky black fur between his ass cheeks. I pulled my foreskin over Colton's head and began to stroke our cocks. Colton pushed his left middle finger in the pup's asshole and massaged his prostate until his precum was dripping on the floor. "Look Kent, the pup didn't get neutered," Colton said and laughed. I looked into Colton's face and I knew he was enjoying the sounding and stroking while his finger was buried inside a tight ass. "Babe I'm gonna cum, I'm gonna cum now," Colton yelled and his seed traveled from his cock through the hollow steel rod into my cock. This took me over the edge and I released my sperm load. My cum pushed Colton's semen back out of my dick, through the sound into his cock, where our two loads mixed together. Colton had our two cum loads inside his cock. We pulled the rod out of our dicks. "Where did the cum go," I asked Colton. "I don't know, it's probably stuck in the tubing somewhere," he answered.

In the meantime two guys got busy in the sling. Colton was planning to give a demonstration on how to humiliate, edge and milk a man. From a hook on the ceiling he had a rope hanging down. A hairy stud with a hot cock and low hanging bull balls was hanging from the rope, his arms tied behind his back. Colton put a red gag into the guy's mouth so he wouldn't scream too loud when he got milked. Colton hit the guy's dick head, using a thin bamboo stick. I heard a muffled scream, coming from the stud. I worked on his ass hole, fucking him with a baseball bat. Colton kept working on his cock. With his right thumb and index finger he rubbed up and down the guy's cock head. "The sooner you give me your cum, the sooner I can use it as a lube on your cock," Colton said. "But remember your dick head will be sensitive after you cum and believe me, I won't stop milking until I get at least three loads out of you. Don't even ask me to stop." Colton didn't have to wait long for the first cum load. He held his hand underneath the guy's dick and collected the semen on his hand. After the milkee was done squirting, Colton grabbed his cock with his fist and stroked it hard, lubing it up well with the hot fresh sperm. The poor guy screamed and tried to pull his cock away from Colton's fist. But his fist was holding on tight and kept stroking the sensitive head, milking the next load out of those big hairy bull balls. The guy was sweating and begging to stop, but Colton just smacked his nuts every time he begged him to stop. I was still fucking the milkee with the baseball bat. His ass juices were oozing out and made an excellent lube. With one forceful push, I slammed the wooden baseball bat deep into his ass. That caused the guy to ejaculate his second load, but that time it sprayed on the dungeon floor. A lean young tattooed stud scooped it up from the floor, using his fingers. He also used it as lube on his cock. He must've been so excited about another man's cum on his cock, he emptied his nuts immediately. He shot his cum on the guys dick, who was fucking someone in the sling, adding his own homemade lube. In the meantime the cute little pup was put on a chain and hooked to a chair. A hairy guy plugged a rubber puppy tail into his ass. I could hear the boy breathing sharply, when he pushed the big plug part inside his hole. It filled the pups tight ass well. Someone manhandled the pup's dick and ball sack from behind with his black leather boots.

"Hey all you horny guys, how about we put the pup in the sling and y'all run a train on him," someone shouted. The pup was dragged to the sling. He laid on his back with the pup tail still wagging in his ass. The first man fucking him pulled the tail out. "Damn that plug stretched his fucking pup hole to the max," the man said. "I have to wait a few if I want it nice and tight. But what the hell, ass is ass," and he pushed his cock inside the boy's pink and stretched hairy ass. When the guys were done seeding the pup hole, Colton said : "Now push it all out, all twelve fucking slimy loads, push it, come on. Give us back our seed."

The boy's hole opened up and the semen of twelve men was gushing out. The tattooed guy was holding a glass bowl underneath his freshly fucked ass and most of the twelve loads splashed into it. He held the bowl up above his head and announced :"Guys, we're gonna have a circle jerk. The first guy shooting his load can drink all the cum in the bowl after each of us nutted his seed into it. So who is the lucky bastard? Go ahead guys, time is starting now."

Everybody was whacking their dicks like there was a gold trophy to win. I didn't believe it, but my Dad was the first one who unloaded his white hot gold. He shot it into the bowl and one after another gave up his seed. Dad was about to drink 15 loads. "Dad if you drink all this, you gonna piss cum for the next two days," I said into the crowd. Dad put the bowl to his mouth and emptied it in one big gulp. Everybody applauded when the bowl was empty.

"Thank you guys, y'all left a pleasant taste in my mouth," he said.

I couldn't believe my Dad was such a kinky pig. That night I also saw Colton's kinky side for the first time. It turned me on seeing him like that. Around 4 am everybody had left.

"That was some hot filthy shit tonight," I said to Colton.

"I'm glad you liked it babe."

The next day we had to clean up the playroom, or dungeon as Colton called it. I took special care of the floor. I made sure all the cum that was spilled was personally removed by myself. It turned me on and I was actually cleaning the floor with a stiff fuck pole.

"You're a sick fucker babe," Colton said and laughed.

The following month I quit my job. Everything was fine between Colton and me. We got along great and Mercedes moved out. We had the entire place to ourself.

We were planning a trip to the Keys. It was only a 3 hour drive to Key West from our house. We wanted to get married there. We had set the date for our marriage on Colton's birthday, August 10th. We both were excited about it and couldn't wait until we would be husband and husband. I decided to take Colton's last name, Sabel.

We left on August 9th early in the morning and arrived at the gay resort in Key West around 11 am. The guy at the front desk was sitting on a chair and was wearing only blue tight shorts. When we walked in, he checked out Colton's ass and crotch. He didn't even do it discreetly. I saw the outlines of his nut sack and cock. His dick started to shift and slowly got bigger.

"Morning," I said to him. "We have a reservation for Colton and Kent Sabel." I thought I use my new last name already since it was only 24 hours until the legal change took place anyway. "Good morning guys," he said, still looking at Colton's body. "Let me see what room I got available. I have only one pool facing room left. The other rooms are facing the parking lot. The problem is I promised the poolside room to someone else. But there is a possibility that this could change."

"Oh yeah ? How and when," I asked.

"Your husband is a very attractive and sexy stud by the way. 10 minutes alone with him could change a lot of things. It's up to you guys." I didn't believe he offered us the better room for having sex with my husband. I jumped behind the front desk and grabbed him by his throat. With my left hand I pinched and twisted his nippel. "Listen you creep, I kill, when it comes to my husband. Is that clear enough for your single digit IQ ?"

"Baaabe, let him go. I'm gonna deal with him. You go to the room and wait there for me. Ok ?"

"What are you gonna do? You give him what he wants. I'm not going anywhere."

"Babe your jealousy is flattering but totally inappropriate. You know you can trust me, I would never hurt your feelings just for a meaningless fuck with a stranger. Ok Mr. Whatever your name is, I want to talk to your manager right now." "I'm Jerome." The guy called the manager on his phone and after two minutes he came into the lobby.

"Hey man," Colton said to him, "your coworker here insulted my husband and me by offering a better room if I have sex with him."

"Dude, I'm sure you're used to that, I bet guys hitting on you all the time. I mean you're a fucking hot looking dude, man. But to make you happy I will give you the poolside room."

We finally went to our room.

"Wow babe, look, there's even a sling hanging from the ceiling," I said with amazement. "We have to celebrate your birthday in that beauty."

"Oh we will, believe me, we will," Colton said in his calm, charming voice.

We unpacked and jumped in the pool. The resort was nicely maintained with lush tropical plants and a Tiki bar by the pool. But everybody was checking out somebody. Me and my jealousy, I guess a gay hotel wasn't really the right place for us to stay. I had to learn to trust Colton. He was not a cheater, I knew that.

The news about me choking the guy in the lobby, traveled around quickly. But it was twisted by the time it reached the second or third person. I found out I was the hero of the day at the resort, when a guy at the pool was talking to me. "Hey, are you the guy who beat up the receptionist to get a better room ?" I didn't correct him. I let everybody believe what they wanted and enjoyed the reputation of being a mean asshole who beats up other people to get his way. Colton must have heard the story too because he smiled when he came back from the Tiki bar, where he got two drinks for us.

"Hey you criminal, I heard what you did. I have second thoughts about getting married to you," he said and laughed. We had a few drinks and I got so drunk, I couldn't make it to the bathroom. I barfed right there at the pool deck. Now I was the mean drunk, who also beats up his partner at home. Oh well. Colton guided me back to the room and put a bucket next to my bed, just in case.

"I think I can't fuck you tonight babe, I'm so sorry," Colton said and laughed.

"If you go in that sling, you probably get sick again from the fuck motion and puke all over the place," he joked.

"Nah, I will be ok by then. It's our wedding eve, we have to fuck. I mean make love," I corrected myself.

"Yeah, I was just kidding babe. I need to go back outside and clean up the mess you made," Colton said to me.

I loved him so much. He did everything for me.

I took a nap to sleep off my buzz. It was almost dinner time when I woke up. Colton was still outside at the pool. He saw me through the window moving around and came inside.

"Hey get your ass ready babe, you gonna get it now," he said when he walked in.

"Oh you are so classy. I'm hungry now, but not for your dick, for food," I said.

"Ok, let's go out for dinner or actually we should just order something. That way you can't beat up somebody again, you drunk criminal," Colton said and smiled.

We ordered Chinese food and were eating outside in front of our room.

Later when it was dark, we went for a walk on Duval street, Key West's main tourist shopping street.

"Too bad we missed the sunset tonight but we can watch it tomorrow, when we are Mr. Colton and Kent Sabel," I said.

The appointment for our wedding was at 10 am on August 10th and we had room number 10. It seemed like a good omen, I would've been more worried if it was 13.

We arrived at the clerk's office 10 minutes earlier. Colton paid our dues and we filled out the paperwork. After we took care of that, the clerk went into a different room with us. There were about 20 chairs and an altar with a cross on top of it.

We both stood in front of the altar and the clerk began to read the vows to us.

Colton and Kent, please face each other and repeat after me.

Colton, I come here today to join your life for years,

I pledge to be true to you, to respect you,

and to grow with you through the years.

May only those best qualities continue to shine

And may our bond continue to grow stronger

I vow here today that this love will be my only love from this day forward.

Then she repeated the same for Colton.

Kent, I came here today....

I looked into Colton's eyes when he repeated the vows. I was in tears and when he saw it, he was too.

MAY I PLEASE HAVE THE RINGS.

Colton, what I have to give you is the promise to take you as my only love from this day forward.

Take this ring, and be part of my life forever.

Kent, what I have to give you....

The wedding ring is a symbol of the vows taken here today.......a circle of wholeness perfect in form. The unending circle of a ring is a sign of fidelity, the pledged faithfulness of a couple to each other. These rings mark the beginning of an unending journey together.

Colton and Kent, if there is anything you remember of this marriage ceremony, remember the love that brought you here today.

Colton and Kent, as you have consented together in lawful wedlock and exchanged your first gifts as a married couple and by the powers vested in me as a Justice of the Peace for the State of Florida, I now pronounce you are now married!

If you wish to seal this marriage with a kiss, you may now do so.

Sure as hell I wanted to seal it with a kiss. I pressed my lips on Colton's and opened my mouth.

"Don't you dare and stick your tongue in my mouth you pig, not here at least," Colton mumbled as good as he could with my lips still on his.

"That's it babe, we are now married," I said to Colton, when we left the clerk's office.

"Yep, it was one of the best and most emotional moments in my life," Colton said.

We drove back to the hotel and got naked.

"Do I get my wedding fuck today or do I have to divorce you already," I joked with Colten. "You could've had it yesterday already if you weren't such a drunk pig," Colton said.

"Smartass."

Colton took me in his arms and we hugged each other for the first time as a married couple.

My hands wandered down to his butt. I sucked on his lips and entered his mouth with my tongue. This time he didn't complain. Our dicks were rubbing on each other and we both got hard.

"I love you so much Colton, I'm so glad you fucked my Dad."

"What ?" Colton asked. "Yeah,otherwise we never would have met," I said.

"That's true but you have a weird way of saying things baby boy. But don't worry, I love you anyway."

We fell on the bed, Colton was on top of me. He lifted my legs up and his cock tried to find it's way to my fuck canal. Colton was holding his dick and circled around my hole with the head.

"Are you ready for your husband's cock babe ? I'm gonna give it to you. Take it," Colton whispered. I felt his head spreading my hole apart, followed by his shaft. His chest was laying on my chest, his balls were hanging on my balls and his hands were holding my hands. He pumped his dick faster into my ass and I knew he wouldn't last much longer. We kissed each other and kept our lips locked together when he stopped humping and filled me up with his load. He took my cock in his hand and pulled my foreskin back. With his left hand he polished my head at the tip. I felt my sperm coming and I saw my head glistening and covered in foamy precum. "Here it comes babe, take it, it's all for you. "My cum shot on Colton's face. "Damn babe, you had some high pressure built up, didn't you ?"

I nodded and licked my own cum off his face.

"Well, we got that done," I said.

"What ?"

"Our wedding fuck," I answered.

"Oh that, yeah I'm glad that's over," he joked.

"Dumbass. Hey, we wanna go in the jacuzzi when it's dark ?" I asked Colton.

"Sure but why after it's dark ? You know, guys go in there to fool around, especially after dark or late nights. I'm afraid you're gonna beat up some poor guy again just because he brushed my leg accidently. What's the difference between a jacuzzi and a hot tub or spa anyway ? What do they have here ?" Colton asked me.

"There is no difference, just different terms for the same thing. But don't worry, I don't think anybody here is gonna touch you or me. Remember, I'm the mean drunk who beats everybody up," I said.

Around 10 pm we grabbed a towel and walked to the jacuzzi. There were already seven guys sitting in it. Well, I shouldn't say sitting. They all grabbed each other by their dicks and balls or had a finger sticking in someone's ass. "See, I told you Kent. On the other hand, why don't we join in? If we play together, then it's not really like cheating," Colton tried to convince me.

"It is cheating, just a different kind. And what if someone would give me more attention than you or vice versa, what then ? You just fucked the shit out of me anyway babe, we don't wanna spoil you too much."

"Ok, ok, was just a suggestion. I don't know why I even asked. I should've known better," Colton said.

"I'm sorry, I didn't wanna snap at you but you know how I get if it comes to that. Let's go back to the pool, there's no room in the jacuzzi anyway."

We went back to the pool. The water had just the perfect temperature, 86 F.

"Do you wanna go home tomorrow or stay another day," I asked Colton. "We could go to see the Hemingway house and the southernmost point of the continental U.S."

"We can do that babe, sounds good to me," Colton answered.

And that's what we did the next day.

First we went to Ernest Hemingway's house and took the tour. The southernmost point was just down the road from where Hemingway's house was.

"I'm H & H, Hungry and Horny," I said to Colton.

"Then let's get something to eat, you spoiled little brat. I'm actually hungry too."

We found a nice little Diner off the beaten path. Colton ordered his favorite dish he always orders when we're eating out, chicken cordon bleu. I had my favorite,stuffed peppers.

We just drove around and checked out the area that afternoon.

"We need to be at home latest by noon tomorrow babe, I forgot to tell you. We can leave early in the morning or tonight, what do you think ?" Colton asked me.

"Tonight is fine, that way we don't have to get up so early. Why, what is around noon ?" I wanted to know.

"Aw nothing special, I have an appointment." That was all he said about it.

We left Key West around 6 pm.

"That was a nice trip, thanks babe," I said.

"Yeah and we even got married," Colton laughed.

I put my left hand on his leg and worked my way up to his basket between his legs. I massaged his bulge and his dick was growing under my hand. I opened the zipper and pulled his stiffening rod out. I could smell my man's sweaty nuts. "Wow, didn't you take a shower earlier ? I smell your balls over here. I mean I'm not complaining," I said and laughed. "Let me smell your pits babe." I squeezed my nose in his armpit and took a big whiff. "Damn, now I'm even hornier. I better stop this or I have to stroke my dick right now," I said. Colton put his dick back in his pants.

We stopped at a gas station about 90 minutes from home. We needed gas and Colton had to piss badly.

"You go baby girl and piss all you want, I pump the gas in the meantime," I said to Colton.

"Ok. But it's questionable who the girl is. Do I lay on my back and spread my legs or you ?" he said and smiled at me. He went inside the gas station to use the restroom and I took the nozzle off the pump to put gas in the car.

I knew I would be done long before Colton came back, so I waited inside the car for him.

I waited fifteen minutes but he still wasn't back. I moved the car from the pump to a parking spot to make room for other people. The place was pretty busy, even 3 cop cars and an ambulance arrived there, but not to get gas. They ran inside the building. I waited another ten minutes before two cops came back outside and were looking around. They kept walking towards me and stopped at my car.

"Hello Sir, can we ask you a few questions ? Please step out of the car." I got out and figured they wanted to ask me if I had seen anything.

"Sir, what is your name? Do you have a photo ID on you ?"

"Kent Sabel, here is my drivers license."

"Thank you. Do you know Mr Colton Sabel ? Is this his vehicle ?" the cop asked.

"Yes, I'm his partner and this is his car."

I saw a helicopter landing behind the building.

"I'm sorry but I have bad news for you. Colton was severely beaten by three men and has life threatening injuries on his head. It seems like his skull was fractured with a heavy object, probably a baseball bat. He's gonna be airlifted to Biscayne Hospital in Miami. For more detailed information you need to contact the doctor's. The good news is, we have one suspect in custody. But there is something else you should know. The other two suspects are still on the run and could be armed and dangerous. Two witnesses heard one suspect saying, they gonna keep looking for you. Do you have any idea who those suspects are and why they are after you both ? We don't know yet if it is a hate crime or robbery. But we do know, the person we arrested is from Key West. And his two buddies probably too. We may need you to identify the arrested person."

I thanked the cop for the info. The helicopter was leaving for Miami. I panicked, thinking about Colton being in there and fighting for his life. I had to get to Miami as soon as possible. Colton needed me. I got back inside the car and speeded northbound on U.S. 1 to the hospital in Miami. I still had ninety minutes to drive. I figured by the time I get there, they already know more about Colton's injuries.

So many things went through my head on the way to Miami. What if those two guys find me, or Colton wouldn't make it. We just got married one day before. Was this a target or random assault? If they knew us, then I should know them too. But I didn't know anybody in Key West. Except the guys from the hotel. They had our address, phone number, credit card number and license plate. I had to see the guy who got arrested. If he was someone from the hotel, then it would be my fault what happened to Colton just because I couldn't keep my damn mouth shut.

I finally arrived at the hospital. I was afraid to ask about Colton in case it went for the worse. I asked to talk to Colton's doctor. After ten minutes of strenuous waiting, he called me into his office.

"Mr Kent Sabel, if I'm right ?"

"Yes you're right."

"Ok. And you are here for Colton Sabel. I'm sorry I don't have any better news. Coltons injuries are so severe, he has been in a coma since he got here. His skull is fractured and punctured his brain in certain areas. We don't know if or when he comes out of the coma. If he does, he may has to learn certain things again. The surgery is in one hour. We do the best we can."

"As long as he is alive I'm ok with everything. Can I see him ?" I asked the doctor.

The doctor told me Coltons room number. He was in the ICU. I entered his room and sat down on the chair next to the bed. I was holding his hand and gave him a kiss. I looked at him and cried. I heard about people in a coma who can hear or feel things, so I talked to him. I thought in case he can feel me holding his hand, I should make him feel good and hold his dick. There was nobody else in the room, so I didn't see a problem. Sometimes people come out of a coma because they hear or feel a loved one. I put my hand under the cover and reached for his dick. It felt warm and soft as always but he didn't get hard. I moved my hand down to his balls and massaged the area between his nut sack and asshole. Suddenly a nurse came into the room and said: "Maybe it looks different on the monitor than what you're actually doing, but you should keep your hands above the cover." It was the most embarrassing moment in my life. The next day at 12 pm the doorbell rang. Was that the appointment Colton mentioned ? I opened the door and a man from the local Mercedes Benz dealership was standing there. "Hi, I have a wedding gift for Kent Sabel from Colton Sabel." I almost cried. Colton bought me a new car as a wedding gift and now he couldn't be here to see me receiving it. It was a black two door Mercedes 560 SEC. I always fantasized about that car. "Thank you," I said and took the keys and paperwork. I parked it in the empty garage.

The next three month I spent close to 24/7 at the hospital to be close to Colton. When I was at home, I felt lonely without him. Sometimes I hugged his pillow at night and cried. I didn't wash his pillow case so I could still smell his scent. When I was at the hospital, I talked to him and held his hand every day.

It was in November, I will never forget that day, when the hospital called me at 2.30 am. I didn't know if I should answer the phone, I was too afraid of bad news. But I needed to know what happened. I picked up my phone and the nurse said:

"Mr Kent Sabel ? I'm calling you in regard to your brother Colton Sabel."

"No he's my husband, not my brother," I corrected her.

"Oh, I'm sorry. Colton came out of the coma ten minutes ago and he asked for you. That means he can remember things."

I told her I will be there shortly.

I don't think I have ever been out of bed that quick. An half hour later I was at the hospital and went straight to Colton's room.

He was halfway sitting up in his bed. When he saw me he smiled and had tears in his eyes.

"Hey baby girl." It was the last thing I said to him three month ago when he went to the restroom at that gas station.

I can't describe how happy I was.

His voice didn't sound the same and he talked differently. But on the other hand, he just came out of a coma.

"I'm so glad to see you. I woke up in this room. Where am I and why am I here ? What happened ?"

"Do you remember when we drove back home from Key West and stopped at that gas station ?"

"Oh yeah. The guy from the hotel was there with his friends.They wanted to have a foursome with me. That's all I remember."

"They were there ?" I asked him.

We kissed each other and were holding hands. He looked and acted so vulnerable. Under normal circumstances it would've been so cute.

"Can I go home with you ? I mean only if it doesn't bother you. Someone told me I would be a nuisance for you."

"Who said that ?" I asked him. I noticed more symptoms of possible brain damage as longer as I was there. I hoped it would pass and all he needed was time to heal.

"Of course I want you to come home. You have to tell the cops about the guys from the hotel, that you saw them and they almost killed you."

"Oh no, they just wanted a foursome. They like it rough, they said. They also wanted to find you to join in. I told them I won't do it because I don't cheat on you. Do you believe me ? I guess you hate me now. Please don't hate me. Everybody else hates me already and wants me to die," Colton said.

It was worse than I thought.

"Nobody hates you babe, I love you more than anything else." He started crying and I knew he didn't believe me. The doctor told me I could take him home. They gave him a prescription to treat his psychosis. If it would help in his case was uncertain.I just had to make sure he takes his meds.

"Hey Colton get up, I can take you home right now," I said to him.

"Why are you doing this to me, I thought you're my friend. I have no friends no more. I'm a bad person but I promise I didn't do a foursome with those guys," Colton kept saying and cried again. "I know you didn't babe. You're not a bad person. I love you." I was sure he would get better again, it just takes a while. I packed his stuff and put him in a wheelchair to roll him outside to the car.

We drove home but Colton was too withdrawn to see and notice his house and everything. He had no facial expressions at all.

"We're home babe," I said when we drove through the gate. We left that place together three month ago

and finally we returned together again.

"Yeah we're home. You didn't meet anybody else in the meantime, did you ?" Colton asked me. Even though I knew he was sick and about the condition he was in, it still was hurting me, that he was thinking that way.

"Of course not, you know me and my jealousy, how could I cheat on you ever, especially when you're in the hospital." I said.

I made dinner for us and gave Colton his meds. It felt so good to have that "We" feeling again.

"You horny baby," I asked him after dinner. "I am definitely sexually deprived." He didn't answer me, he was too withdrawn again. I was sure the meds made him kinda drowsy. He went to bed right after dinner and fell asleep. I wanted to kill that guy from the hotel in Key West. The police still didn't have any trace of the two accomplices. The guy they had arrested was out on bail bond. I looked for the phone number of the hotel and found it on the receipt. I called the hotel and hoped for the manager or the other guy to answer the phone. I got lucky. The guy I choked, Jerome, was answering.

"Gay Resort Happy Ocean Waves," he said in his gayish provocative voice. "How can I help you ?"

"You can only help me if you kill yourself, you fucking faggot, by choking to death on the next dick you suck. Guess what, Colton recognized you guys. It's just a matter of time when you go to jail," I told him. He didn't say a word before he hung up.

I also went to bed early and snuggled up to Colton. I was already horny but feeling Colton's body so close made it even worse. I had to jerk off at least. My dick got hard and I rubbed it against Colton's ass cheeks. The medication put him in a deep sleep, he didn't show any signs of waking up. With my left arm I reached around him and played with his soft cock. My dick was throbbing. What would happen if I stick my dick in his ass, I thought to myself. Would he wake up ? He told me a while ago he never got fucked. I would've been the first one if I had fucked him that night and he wouldn't even know about it, except he would wake up. I was too horny not to try and the temptation was too much. I put a big scoop of Vaseline on my dick and spread Colton's ass cheeks apart. My cock head found its way to his soft pink hairy hole on its own . All I had to do was push it in. My dick slid in Colton's man cave with no resistance. Damn babe you are loose for someone who never got fucked before, I thought. I heard Colton moaning and he pushed his ass back against my crotch, pushing my pole in even deeper. Was he awake or was it just a reflex ? I started pumping back and fore, rubbing my head against the smooth lining inside of his fuck tunnel. I let the juice of my loins flow into Colton, flooding his virgin ass. "I love you baby," I whispered in his ear."

"Love you too baby boy," Colton answered. I was stunned. He was awake.

"You're awake ?"

"Sure. Do you think I sleep through an event like that ? I gave you my seed, now I wanted yours. I never asked you for it because I thought you don't like being top," he said. "I only like topping you," I answered.

I pulled my dick out of Colton, but held my hand underneath it to catch my cum in case it would leak out of his butt.

Colton got up before I did the next morning. "My asshole hurts," was the first thing he complained about.

"Another quick fuck would ease the pain," I told him.

"Don't even think about it. I don't know how you bottoms do it all the time, but this girl can't do it. Don't get me wrong, I loved having you and your cum inside of me. Speaking about your cum, it's still in there," Colton said.

He seemed to be doing better than the night before. Maybe the meds helped already.

"Hey Colton, I may have to visit an old friend today but I will be back before five, ok ? I'll take the Corvette if you don't mind."

"Ok, I'm gonna get some rest in the meantime, I'm still feeling kinda dizzy," he said.

I took a friend of mine with me to Key West that day. I used him as bait for this Jerome guy from the hotel. We drove to the hotel and my friend Jay went inside the lobby.

"Hi, why is a handsome man like you by himself on such a fabulous day," Jerome said.

"Well, why don't you keep me company and show me a few places if you don't mind," Jay responded.

"Oh I would love to," he said in his queenish voice. "I actually get off work in 30 minutes. Do you need a room for tonight ?" We have one available for only 80 bucks."

"Aw, no thanks. That's too much. But I will meet you outside in 30 minutes. I'm in the red Corvette," Jay told him.

Jay came back outside and got on the driver seat. I had to get behind the seat which was a tight squeeze in a Corvette with no back seat. After about 25 minutes, Queen Jerome, that's how I called him, finally came outside and jumped on the passenger seat.

"Wow, that's a fancy car, I like it. But it has no back seat. Where do you fuck if you have someone in here ?" Jerome said. I had a cover on top of me so he wouldn't see me. Jay asked him "You know a quiet place where we can fuck ? Maybe in the woods with no people around ?"

"Oh yeah, I know a lot of places in the woods, I'm a slutty girl," Jerome said and laughed. It made my stomach hurt just listening to that slut. Jay drove to a nearby wooded area where Jerome told him to go. He parked right next to a tree, so close that Jerome couldn't open the door. I pulled the cover of me, threw it around Jerome's neck and tied it behind the back rest of his seat. He was unable to move his head or chest. He started screaming "Help, I'm being raped by a murderer."

"You wish you dirty little whore. I wouldn't fuck you even if I get paid for it. But I would fuck you up like you and your buddies did my husband Colton," I said to him. He was so scared, he was shaking. I climbed to the front and was sitting on Jerome's lap. I pulled a knife out of the glove compartment and held it to his throat. He pissed his pants when he felt the cold steel blade on his skin. "Oh, that pig is pissing on Colton's seat. He won't be happy about that at all. You better clean it up," I yelled at Jerome. I told Jay to stay out of everything so he wouldn't get in trouble. He moved the car away from the tree so I could open the door and have better access to Jerome. I pulled his shoes, socks and pants off. His shirt I cut open with the knife and ripped it off. He was completely naked. I put handcuffs around his wrists and a dog collar on his neck. I hooked a long chain to the collar and tied him to a tree. Then I made him clean up the seat, licking his own piss off the leather while I smashed his cell phone against a tree. "Ok you slut, I heard you wanted to get fucked, is that right ?"

"No, no I changed my mind. Please let me go. I'm too young to die. If you let me go I will turn myself in and my buddies," Jerome begged.

"Who said you're gonna die, you idiot ? That would be too good for you," I yelled at him again. I walked around the car and took a steel pipe out of the trunk. It was about as thick as two of my fingers. I stepped in front of Jerome and held the pipe over my head.

"I should just smash it in your fucking head like you guys did to Colton. Now go down on your hands and knees you whore. I don't want you to be disappointed when I leave. You wanted to get fucked, I fuck your queeny ass in my own way. You won't forget that one, believe me," I said to him. I was so angry at this moron, I had to be careful not to do anything stupid that could put me in prison. I stepped behind Jerome and lined the steel pipe up to his asshole. I didn't put any lube on it to make it hurt even more but I couldn't push it in. His shithole didn't stretch open from being too scared I thought.

I remembered I had one quart of motor oil in the trunk. I opened the bottle and dipped the pipe into the oil. Half of the oil I poured on his scrawny ass. I held the pipe to his fuckhole again and pushed it in as hard as I could. "Open up you stupid fucker," I yelled and finally the pipe disappeared in his rectum. He screamed louder than anybody else I heard before. I pushed and pulled the pipe in and out of his ass. A few times I pulled it out completely to ram it back in, each time harder than before. With my other hand I grabbed him by his nuts and squeezed as hard as I could. It almost took his breath. "Shut the fuck up or I will give you a real reason to scream," and I kicked his nuts hard from behind with my steel toed work boot. He passed out from the plow in his ball sack. I took a few pictures of him laying there naked and passed out in the dirt to show them to Colton. The steel pipe was still sticking in his ass and both of his hands were cupping his nuts.

I left him there as he was. I took his clothes and threw them into a lake not far from the scene.

"Ok Jay, job done well. We can go back home now." Three hours later we pulled into the garage at home.

"You wanna come in and say hi to Colton," I asked Jay. He and Colton had never met before.

"Sure why not. I was curious about your husband since you started telling me about him."

We went inside and I called Colton.

"Hey babe I'm back." He was laying on the couch in the living room and had his cell phone in his hand.

"I wanna introduce you to my friend Jay."

"Hey Jay, nice to meet you. Have you been with Kent in the past four or five hours ?"

"Yes, longer than that actually."

"Well the cops just called me and said Jerome Myers in Key West pressed charges against Kent for assault with a weapon and a few other things. But I can't believe that Kent would hurt anybody with a weapon," Colton said.

"Babe I have to tell you something. I also took a few pics. Here, that's Jerome Myers. I went down to Key West and scared the little queenie bitch. He is the one in the hotel who beat the crap out of you. Well, his buddies did but he is one of the accomplices. You have to tell the cops that he is one of them. I can't believe he was that stupid and talked to the cops."

Colton looked at the pics and smiled.

"Yes, that's him. Definitely him. Is that pipe sticking where I think it is," Colton asked and laughed.

"Yes it is. He wanted to get fucked, so I fucked him. He told Jay to pick him up after work. It was all consensual. He even wanted me to get kinky and cut his shirt open, that weird tramp. Jay is my witness. And when you tell the police that he is one of them who beat you up, I have nothing to worry about."

"Yeah I hope so. The cops asked if you were home. There's a warrant out for your arrest," Colton told me.

20 minutes later the cops were at the gate. Jay was leaving and on his way out he let the cops in. They put me in handcuffs and I thought it was funny because a few hours before I handcuffed Jerome.

"Are you Kent Sabel ? There are accusations and charges pressed against you for assault with a weapon," the cop said to me.

"But it was consensual," I told him.

Colton told the officer about the incident at the gas station and that Jerome Myers is one of the suspects they were looking for.

"Now that makes sense. Your assault on Mr Myers doesn't look like consensual sex, it looks more like getting even for what he and his friends did to Mr Colton Sabel," the officer said to me.

"I have a warrant for your arrest. You have to go to county jail. You are under arrest."

Colton was getting ready to pick me up in jail after he paid for my bail bond.

"I see you later babe," I said to Colton when I left the house.

The booking process in jail took three hours. I was in a holding cell until I was done with booking. By then Colton should've been there to bail me out, but he wasn't. They put me in a pod with 14 cells. I was nervous and scared, it was the first time for me being in jail. Because I had assault charges, I was in the same pod as inmates who were incarcerated for murder. I had one free 30 second phone call to call Colton. But he didn't answer his phone. In every cell were two beds and one mattress on the floor because the jail was overfilled. I was sitting on my mattress and was worried about Colton. Something must've happened. At eleven pm the lights were turned off but I couldn't sleep. At 4 am the c/o, or correctional officer, rolled breakfast in on big carts. It was actually pretty good, cereal with chocolate milk and a piece of pound cake to die for. After breakfast, everybody went back to bed until lunchtime at 11 am. We had sausage and beans, they called it the homewrecker. I was just done eating when the c/o called my name and yelled through the pod I got bailed out.

One hour later I walked through the door to the parking lot where I expected Colton to pick me up. I saw him waving at me.

"What happened," I asked him when I got in the car.

"I'm sorry, I don't know what happened. I was getting ready to pick you up and when I looked at my phone it was 9 am."

"Oh shit, you probably blacked out. I won't leave you alone any more. I should've known better.

Let's go home and relax. You know, we should take your wedding gift for a spin tomorrow. You didn't even see it yet."

"That would be nice," Colton said.

"I hope I don't have to go to jail. You can't be by yourself, not yet."

My court date was set for December 6th. They arrested the other two suspects, including Jerome for conspiracy.

Colton's medication was working great. He showed almost no symptoms. Only sometimes I noticed a slight difference in his behavior.

"Oh damn, Kent I forgot to tell you, Mercedes and her boyfriend are gonna stop by tonight. I never met the guy. I'm curious if he's really that great. She always brags about him."

"Yeah, all she brags about is his dick," I said to Colton.

"Let's hang out at the pool and if they show up they can join us. At least we get to see him in his swim trunks. That's the best way to see how hung he is built down there," I said.

Late afternoon Mercedes and her boyfriend showed up in a white stretched Lincoln Towncar Limo.

They came to the pool and had a few drinks with us.

"What's about the Limo," Colton asked his daughter.

"Dad, we came over to tell you something. I didn't wanna tell you over the phone. Dad, Charlie and I got married."

I almost choked on my drink.

"Is the white Limo supposed to imply something or they didn't have a different color ?" I asked her as a joke. She didn't answer my question and seemed a little upset about my question but I was sure she knew what I meant.

Colton was sad because his only daughter didn't tell him about her wedding. She was afraid he wouldn't approve her decision.

Charlie didn't wanna go in the pool at first but changed his mind after a few drinks. He was tall, clean shaven and had no body hair at all. He had blond long hair to his shoulder and a short ponytail. Not my type at all. He took his clothes off and jumped naked in the pool.

"Seems like he's not a shy person," I said to Mercedes.

"No he's pretty open minded," she answered, whatever that meant. I was curious if his dick was really as big as Mercedes always told us. It was hard to see his size in the water. I had to wait until he got out of the pool. Colton cuddled up to me behind the waterfall in one corner of the cave. After a while Charlie came through the waterfall into the cave, which gave me and Colton a good sight at his dick. His cock looked like it was hard and pointed up his belly in a 45° angle. I thought it must be the reflection of the water that made it look that big. Colton and I looked at each other and didn't know what to expect. "Hey fellas, how's it hanging? Sorry about my dick, it always gets hard when I'm naked in public as you guys can see." He came very close to us and stood right next to me with his drink in one hand. With his other hand he started playing on his horse cock. He tried to put his drink on a floating cup holder behind me, when I felt his cock brushing against my leg. I acted like I didn't notice anything. When he was behind me to put his drink on the cup holder, he put his huge boner on my ass and tried to get it in my hole. I jumped forward to get away from him. I felt my own cock stiffening but I tried to hide it.

"You can't do that Charlie. Because we are gay doesn't mean we fuck everything we can get. We're married and faithful to each other and what would Mercedes say if she sees her Dad naked and hard together with her husband ?" Colton said to Charlie.

"Sorry guys. You are no fun. What's wrong with you? My cock is bigger than both of yours together you motherfucking bastards." I was about to punch his face.

"Let him go Kent, he's drunk," Colton said. He was always so understanding and calm.

I gave Charlie his drink and a hard push towards the waterfall.

"Get away from us or I knock your fucking teeth out, you won't call me names no more you bastard," I yelled at him. Mercedes heard the yelling and checked on us. "What happened, why is Charlie naked ?" she asked.

"Nothing, he's just drunk and tripping over his own feet. You should bring him home," I told her.

She took his arm and helped him to get out of the pool and into the passenger seat in her car. They left five minutes later after she struggled to put his pants back on.

"Well so much for our relaxing afternoon," I said.

"But to be honest babe, that horse cock made my dick twitch and now I'm horny as fuck," I said to Colton.

"Yeah you're always horny. But it was hot to watch when he grabbed you and tried to stick that horse cock in your poor little ass," Colton said and grabbed his dick.

We went back to the same spot in the cave where Charlie tried to rip me apart. "Imagine you're a big bad sea monster and you want me so bad your legs are shaking, your cock is throbbing and aching to get drained in my little virgin fuckhole," I said to Colton and laughed.

"Virgin fuckhole, my ass," he laughed. I saw Colton's dick getting bigger.

"Damn babe, did that big bad sea monster fantasie turn you on," I joked with him.

"Yes. The big bad sea monster needs to breed his mermaid," he said in his deep manly voice. I pulled my trunks off and swam closer to Colton. I stripped him naked as well and teased his cock by rubbing my ass cheeks against him.

"Wow baby, I just remembered you haven't cum in three month. No wonder your cock is rigid like a teenager's dick," I said and took his fuck tool in my hand and guided it to my willing hole, hungry for Colton's sperm piston. He rammed it in with no mercy but I didn't care. All I wanted was to feel Colton's cock, I wanted his dick to hurt me, to remind me there is no pain with Colton, just unconditional love and lust.

His thrusts got harder and created low waves, splashing against the cave walls. He pulled his cock out of me. His Left hand reached through my legs and grabbed my cock from behind and pulled it backwards. Colton rubbed his cock head against mine and his load sprayed into the blue pool water and floated in stringy little clouds around my cock. I felt my own jizz boiling inside my shaft. I turned around and stuck my loaded cock between Colton's hairy thighs and nut sack, where I released my semen. Colton tried to catch my floating cum with his hands and was even successful. He licked it off his hands and said: "The big bad sea monster is eating your little mermaid babies."

He was so cute when he said this. I kissed his lips and tasted my cum.

We went inside the house and he made a pizza for us.

"Hey Colton, you told me a while ago you have electro stim equipment down in the dungeon. I wanna try it some time."

"Sure, why not after dinner ?"

"Nah, I need to be in the mood for it. I'm not horny enough right now because the big bad sea monster just ate all my babies. Maybe tomorrow," I said.

But the next day we got up early. We both were horny again and our cocks were alternating between morning wood and softie. We wanted to take my new car for a ride. Colton never drove in it until that morning. I put only 800 miles on it since I got it. Colton usually uses his Corvette or the Jaguar. He still had his father's old Rolls Royce in the garage but he didn't have it registered.

We put only shorts and a t-shirt on and got in my car. We drove to the beach and to a few parks. I drove slowly through the last park we visited. I opened my zipper and pulled my balls and dick out and started stroking.

Colton did the same, he was also too horny to just watch me stroking and waiting until we got home. We noticed a few single males driving around or parking for a while, walking into the woods and coming back after a few minutes.

"Let's park over there and see what happens," I said to Colton. We parked there for about five minutes and played with our dicks. A white work van stopped not far from us. The driver got out and walked in our direction. He was a dark tanned construction worker with tattoos on his arms and wearing a baseball cap. He stopped right next to my door and rubbed his dick through his pants. The outline of his meat grew bigger. We didn't stop stroking our cocks. He pulled his cock out and got fully erect. He was uncut and his foreskin looked very tight around his head, too tight to even pull it back.

I asked him how he is cleaning his dick under his foreskin. He told us he pulls his skin back only once a week to have his cock head cleaned by a professional. He said:"You fuckers are lucky, today is day five after cleaning."

He pulled his foreskin slowly back, slow enough not to hurt himself or rupture his tight skin. A strong smell of male muskiness lingert over to us, a smell only a man has under his foreskin.

"My buddy shows up any minute, if you guys wanna watch him cleaning my cock you're very welcome," he said to us.

We decided to give it a try. We could watch them and jerk off. There was his buddy, parking his motorcycle next to the van. They both got in the back of the van and left the door cracked open. We walked over to the open van door and got inside. The biker took the construction guy's foreskin in his mouth and sucked on it to make it soft and easier to pull back, so he said. After a few minutes he started to peel the skin back with his thumb and index finger. The strong smell filled out the small area in the van very quickly and it smelled even stronger. He took the construction worker's dirty cock head in his mouth and licked all the white cheese off.

The construction guy started talking dirty:"Lick my head cheese off my dirty cock head you biker whore. Pull my fucking skin back and make it hurt." The biker licked and sucked on the head until there was nothing left of the white gooey man cheese. With one hard pull the biker pulled the guy's foreskin all the way back over his head and made him grunt in pain. The same second he shot his cum all over the bikers face. Colton and I were so horny from watching the hot scene, we came at the same time and unloaded our cocks also on the bikers face.

"Well in five days you guys can watch our cleaning ceremony again if you want," the construction worker said.

We both felt a lot better after shooting our cum on the bikers face. We were thinking about coming back in five days.

But the day of my court date also came terribly close. I met with my lawyer two days before court. She said because it was my first offense I would most likely get probation. And the judge would take the fact in consideration, that I have to care for Colton after those scumbags beat him half to death. I was kinda relieved after talking to my lawyer but waiting until the 6th was still nerve wrecking.

Monday, December 6th was a chilly day. Colton was even wearing a jacket when we left for my court date at 9 am. We were sitting on a bench in the second row in the courtroom. The judge was an elderly cranky looking woman. My lawyer called her the pit bull.

"She's a bitch, between me and you. You never know what you get with her," my lawyer said to me.

"Well great, that's all I need. A cranky judge."

I asked my lawyer in case there is something unexpectedly going wrong, if it would be possible to have Colton step up to the judge's bench and tell her the circumstances and his point of view why I did what I did. I did it for Colton.

"She's not the most gay friendly person," my lawyer said.

But I still had hope. Colton is a good talker, calm, understanding, convincing and to the point. I would actually rely more on him than on my lawyer. Around 10.30 am my name was called.

"It will be alright baby," Colton said.

The judge started to talk after my lawyer and I stepped up to the bench.

"Mr. Kent Sabel, you are married to a man, Mr Colton Sabel. Is that right ?"

"Yes, your honor."

"And you did self justice on another person, Mr Jerome Myers ?"

"No your honor."

"I can't even name the brutal things you did to this person Mr Sabel. Your defense is, it was consensual intimacy between you and Mr Myers."

"Yes, your honor."

"I don't understand why Mr Myers is telling the opposite of your story and risked being incarcerated for something you punished him already by going to the police. You Mr Sabel are charged for assault with a deadly weapon, punishable by incarceration of up to five years in a federal prison. Your defense is also that this crime was your first offense and you have to care for Mr Colton Sabel after his hospital stay.

After careful consideration of your defense, I have to sentence you to one year in county jail."

I almost got a heart attack. That bitch called that careful consideration ? Colton turned pale and looked sad. My lawyer asked the judge if Colton could say a few words.

"I don't know what that would change but keep it short," the judge said.

"Your honor, I'm Colton Sabel and I don't think your considerations were quite careful enough. I was a victim of Mr Myers and his friends. Their crime was far worse than what was done to Mr Myers. Mr Myers is known in Key West for his, let's call it, special intimacy practices, or kink as he would say. He is also known to have sex for money. He met with Mr Kent Sabel for sex that day. For kinky sex your honor. Kinky sex are the things you can't even say in this court room. He expected payment from Mr Kent Sabel for kinky sex practices he couldn't even fulfill. Because of him I was in a three month coma and needed my partner at home to take care of me. I can't be around a stranger to take care of me because it causes me to have panic attacks.

Thank you your honor," Colton said.

I already saw me going to jail, when the judge said:"Mr Colton Sabel, I heard your concerns and defense and I was wrong. I thank you so much for speaking up. I sentence Mr Kent Sabel to one year probation."

"I knew it babe, you did it. You should be a lawyer. You always keep me out of trouble or help me out of it. Thank you for loving me."

We left the courthouse after Colton gave his outstanding speech in front of the judge. I was sentenced to one year probation, which is way better than being in jail for 12 month. It was long enough for me, when I had to stay in jail overnight which wasn't even 24 hours.

Once a month I had to see my probation officer. Colton made sure I didn't miss any of my appointments again. I missed one so far. He went to my probation officer and talked to her, to make sure she wouldn't report me. She had a crush on Colton, which made it easier for me. She thought Colton is my older brother who looks out for me. My February appointment was at 2 pm but I couldn't make it on time. We took a power nap and woke up at 2.20 pm

"Colton, you need to call her and explain why I'm late. She does everything you want her to do or not to do actually."

"Yes but in the very near future I have to tell her who I really am. Or I have to fuck her. I don't think that's in your interest Mr. Jealous," Colton told me.

"No but just drag it out as long as you can."

Colton dialed her number and she picked up.

"Hi Mr. Sabel, what did your brother do this time ?"

"Nothing bad, we both just woke up five minutes ago from a nap."

"You should come over to my place this evening and tell me what happened," she laughed.

"See I told you," Colton whispered to me.

"Please babe," I begged.

"Well I don't know about tonight Ms. Flint, any other day ?"

"I have an idea. You and your brother come over tonight and I will move his appointment to 7 pm.

If not, there is nothing I can do."

"Did that bitch just blackmail me or what," Colton said. He told her we both would be there at seven.

"You need to keep your appointments babe, or I have to fuck her, and we both don't want that to happen," Colton said.

We drove over to her house that night. She opened the door in a red short skirt and her t-shirt didn't cover much.

"Hey guys. Wow, Colton, you look even more stunningly handsome tonight. Do you like my outfit ? Kent, you only have to sign the timesheet and you are free to go. Your brother and I have some serious business to do," she said. Colton looked at me because he was afraid I would get jealous any second. And I did. I had to put her in her place.

"You're one of those females who think they can get every man by just lifting a skirt and showing their hairless skinny legs. Aren't you? But not with me. I can see right through you. You better don't touch Colton."

"What's wrong with him ? I just did him a big favor and he's insulting me. Your brother is old enough to know what he's doing," she said.

"Are you a natural blond or what ?" I yelled at her. "Babe be quiet now. You know you always get upset too easily," Colton said to me and then he turned to Ms. Fink again.

"I apologize for Kent Ms. Fink. He has a medical condition called OJD, Obsessive Jealousy Disorder."

"Oh the poor guy, I never heard about it," she said.

"Every Time somebody wants to touch me he freaks out," Colton told her.

"Is that why you called him baby, to calm him down ?" she asked.

"Ah no, not exactly. I call him baby because he's my husband, and to calm him down too." She looked at Colton and said : Husband ? What do you mean ?"

"We are legally married Ms. Fink. We are both gay," Colton finally told her.

She had a disappointed look on her face. She turned around and went into her bedroom but left the door cracked open. She didn't say anything. Colton and I just looked at each other. "Well I guess we go home," I said to Colton, when we suddenly heard her and two male voices coming from the bedroom. The voices changed into heavy breathing and moaning.

"What kind of a freak is she, she hit on you while two guys were waiting in her bedroom ?" I said to Colton. But the male curiosity in us took over and we sneaked to her bedroom door. Colton pushed it a little bit more open so we could see what's going on in there. We couldn't believe what we saw. She was lying in a sling. One guy had his hand inside her pussy while the other man shoved his cock in her at the same time.

"That's so disgusting. I don't mean watching the two guys, I mean her," I said to Colton.

"Why ? Remember my dick was in a pussy before. I'm a dad. Let's spy on them and jerk off," Colton said.

The guy that was fisting her pussy moved his hand in and out but at the same time he held the other guy's cock in his fist and stroked him off inside her. His fist made her pussy squirt and the juice ran down from her vagina to the black leather between her legs, from there it dripped to the floor and created a small puddle.

Colton and I had our pants around the ankles and stroked our hard cocks. Colton enjoyed himself, he had that bedroom eyes look on his face. He looked so cute and I was glad he had fun. I was turned on by the two guys, but her pussy just creeped me out.

The one guys cock started to spray his seed inside of her, mixing his cum with her fuck cream and covering the other man's fist in a gooey mess. He pulled his hand out and licked it as clean as possible. He rammed his cock in her pussy and bred her for at least another two minutes. It seemed like he was going on and on. Then Colton's cum shot against the door and ran slowly down to the floor. I wiped some of his cum off the floor and stuck my finger in my mouth.

"Mhh babe you taste salty n sweet tonight. What did you eat ?" I whispered in his ear. We both sneaked out of her house and left. I didn't get off but I wanted to save it for Colton when we got home.

I took a short video of her in the sling just in case I screwed up again and missed my probation appointment. She probably wouldn't help me out again, knowing Colton is gay. But with that video I had good chances to get off probation right away.

"You're such a criminal Kent, don't you think it could turn around and bite you in the ass," Colton said.

"No, not really. I have to protect myself and do what's best for me," I answered him.

"Now you sound like a selfish little prick Kent. I love you to death but sometimes I wonder about you," Colton said and sounded disappointed.

But the next day I called her anyway and told her about the video I took of her and the two guys.

"I want you to release me from probation immediately or I have to show this video to your friends and family. Oh, and your employer would be surprised too, don't you think ?"

She agreed and I was off probation the same month.

Colton is a good hearted man but he didn't appreciate some of the things I did. I admired him for how he was interacting with people and dissolving any problem just with words. I have always been a borderline criminal to achieve my goals. But I wanna change for Colton.

I told him that I was done with probation and I would change my behavior. He was standing naked next to the chair I was sitting on. I thought he probably would like me playing with his dick to get him in a better mood.

"Come closer babe, you need a good milking," I said to him and reached over to get a hold of his cock. I massaged and rubbed his head and his precum made it nice and slippery. He was shivering and his knees were shaking. "Yeah babe, let it go. Drop your load on the floor. I will clean it up."

His first cum shot flew high through the air and splashed on my chest, the less forceful shot that followed landed on the floor. I went down on my knees and licked the last drops off the tip of his cock. I held my cock in my right hand and lowered myself enough to wipe Colton's cum off the floor,using only my cock head. His cum had an earthy odor but still the bittersweet taste I love. His cum worked well as a lube on my cock, so I wasn't surprised when I nutted only a few strokes later on my hand. Colton licked it off, leaving my hand wet from his spit.

"Good boy. There's some of my cum in your beard," I said to Colton. I licked it off his beard and gave him a long sloppy kiss, when we exchanged my chewing gum from my mouth to his.

"Damn, only two guys can make such a mess. My chest, hand, floor, our dicks and your beard got covered in our semen," I said and laughed. "Let's take a shower babe or actually let's go in the pool."

We both walked naked to the pool and jumped in. We stood in a corner of the pool. I put my arms around Colton, our dicks rubbed against each other and I kissed him again.

"I love you so much Colton, I will live up to every word I said when I repeated the vows to you."

"That's sweet of you baby, I will do the same," Colton said to me.

A few days later when we drove home from the grocery store, we saw a new adult book store had opened up on 5th Ave. "Hey Colton, we should check that one out. You want to ?" I asked him. "Sure why not," he said.

We parked right in front of the entrance and went inside. We walked through the aisles and checked out the toys. Colton went over to the DVD section and browsed through the discounted ones. There was this guy going in and out of the arcade area where they had the private booths. He kept looking at Colton and checking him out. Colton didn't give him any attention and was still going through the DVD's. But I kept a close eye on him. The guy got closer to Colton and acted like he was interested in the DVD's. I got distracted for a few seconds by another customer squeezing through between me and the shelf. When I looked back over to Colton, the guy had his hand on Colton's ass and kissed him on the mouth. I dropped the double ended dildo I had in my hands and went over to them to help Colton to get rid of the guy. But Colton just stood there and let the guy kiss and fondle him. I was crazy mad in just a matter of seconds. When the guy saw me coming, he stepped away from Colton. Colton knew what was coming. I pushed the guy against the wall, hitting his head against it. I grabbed his balls through his open fly and kept squeezing them hard. The guy screamed and begged me to stop but it made me even more mad. The store clerk came over from behind the register and tried to get me off the guy. "I'm gonna castrate the motherfucking asshole," I yelled at the clerk. He threatened to call the cops if I wouldn't let go of the guy. But if I'm angry I don't care about anything. I screamed at the clerk: "Don't you dare to call the fucking cops or you're the next one who needs plastic surgery."

Colton tried to get me off the guy.

"Kent stop it right now and go outside to the car," Colton yelled.

"Oh look who's talking. You didn't stop him from kissing you. You probably didn't want him to stop. You liked it, didn't you ? Tell me, did you like it ?" I yelled back.

I went on and on when Colton and I went outside to the car.

"You should be happy he didn't press charges against you. Why do you always have to get that violent ? I would've told him to stop but I was too stunned for a few seconds. That's why I was just standing there," Colton explained.

"Yeah, I've seen it. Don't try to lie to me you bastard," I yelled at Colton.

"Did you just call me a bastard ?" Colton asked me.

I didn't answer and we both didn't say anything on our way home. Every time I get angry, I feel sad and bad about what I did a few minutes later. I called my baby a bastard and he was hurt. We got home and he put the groceries in the refrigerator.

"Kent, I want you to do anger management counseling. If you really love me you do that for us."

"I'm so sorry I called you a bastard. I love you more than anything. I do everything you want me to babe. I know I need help with my anger issues. I get so mad I can't control what I'm doing."

Colton saw the tears in my eyes and he knew I was serious about it. I looked up phone numbers of local places I could go for counseling. After a few calls I found the best place for me and made an appointment for the following week. I tried to stay out of trouble as much as I could, that meant to avoid situations where I usually get angry. My first counseling went pretty well. The counselor did an evaluation and created a treatment plan. It seemed easy enough to me. I just had to go every week and soon I would be a better person. I was happy I could help to save our relationship and this was a small price to pay. I would've done anything for Colton.

I heard about a new gay campground not far from us.

"Colton, would you like to go to the new gay campground ? Just for a few hours ?" I asked him.

"I wouldn't mind going but not before you're done with counseling," Colton said.

"Well I already did a few sessions and I promise I won't start anything."

"Kent, you should avoid places like that at all, I'm not going there with you until you finish counseling."

He was right, I should stay home, but it pissed me off that he told me what to do.

"Come on babe, let's go. Just an hour or so. I'm bored," I kept trying to talk Colton into it.

But he didn't go.

"Well then I'll go by myself," I said and left. I just walked around the place and checked it out. It had a heated pool, two bars, Cabins and tent sites. I sat down at the poolside bar and had a few drinks. I was already drunk but still ordered a few more.

"Hey handsome you shouldn't sit here all by yourself," I heard a voice saying from behind me. An older guy stood behind me and put his hand on my shoulder.

"Oh really, I'd rather sit here by myself than with you. Take your dirty paws off me. I'm a married man," I said to him.

"Aw a married man, huh. And where is the husband ? Does he know you're sitting here drunk and looking for dick ?" the guy asked me.

"It's not your fucking business, now leave me alone or I knock your friggin dentures out," I yelled at him. He still stood behind me and kept touching me on my arms and legs. When he grabbed my dick, I lost it. If Colton would've been there, he would keep me from doing something stupid. But he wasn't there and I got in trouble. I swung my fist at the guy's face and hit his nose. He screamed and was holding his nose with his hand. Blood ran down his lips and chin. The bartender called an ambulance. They told me I broke the guy's nose. "I told him to stop grabbing me," I said. I asked the bartender to call Colton and tell him to pick me up. I gave him Colton's number and he called.

"Hi, is this Colton, I'm Chris the bartender at the new campground. Your partner asked me to call you. He's drunk as shit and needs a ride home. He got into a fight with another guest and broke the guy's nose."

"You're kidding me. Ok, tell him I'm on my way," Colton told the bartender. 30 minutes later I saw Colton coming inside the bar.

"I know, I know. I screwed up again. Keep your lecture to yourself and bring my ass home," I said to Colton and slurred my words.

"Don't worry Kent, I won't bother you with my lecture. I'm sick and tired of this bullshit. This is the last time I put up with this," Colton said to me in a loud voice. He was angry.

"Oh yeah, or what ? I don't need you, you fucking asshole," I yelled at Colton.

"And I certainly don't need a violent drunk in my life. You can pick up your stuff tomorrow, I don't wanna see you ever again," Colton yelled back. He turned around and left.

"Man, are you crazy ? This was your husband ? You let this hot, sexy stud leave. That was the stupidest thing you could do. You have a place to crash ? If you want you can stay at my place and we go from there," the bartender said to me.

I accepted his offer and crashed on his couch. The next morning when I woke up I felt horrible. I had a hangover and it became clear to me what I had done last night. I panicked by the thought of losing Colton. Or had I lost him already ?

I kneeled on the floor and cried like a baby, calling Colton's name over and over again. I hurt him once again. The person I loved most I kept hurting most. Chris came out of his bedroom and checked on me. "I feel for you man, if I had that hot stud as a boyfriend and he would break up with me, I would be crying myself."

Chris was a good guy. I could stay at his place as long as I needed to. He gave me mental support and advice. We became very good friends.

I decided to wait until the next day to call Colton. He was probably still too upset to talk to me that morning, just a few hours after the incident. I cried for most of the day. I promised myself never to touch alcohol again and go to all my counseling sessions. I would do anything to be with Colton again. I thought it's probably a better idea to send Colton a text message instead of calling. That way he couldn't hang up on me or interrupt me and he had time to think about what he was answering.

But I couldn't wait until the next day. I sent him a text around 2 pm.

"Colton, I know you're mad at me. I'm mad at myself. I love you so much. I need you in my life. Without you I'm a lost pup. I was drunk and stupid last night. I won't touch alcohol again, I promise. I will go to all my counseling appointments. I want to change my life and become a better person so I can be with you again forever.

Love always

Kent"

I showed the text to Chris before I sent it to Colton, asking if it sounds ok to him.

"That's the most heart wrenching text message I've ever read," Chris said.

I pushed the send button on my phone and waited for Colton's response. But he didn't respond at all. He had to be really hurt. But if he loved me as much as I loved him, how could he not answer my text ? I didn't hear from him for two days. On the second day, when Chris came home from bartending, he smiled at me and said: "Guess who was at the bar today ? Your ex stopped by and ordered a drink."

"Colton ? You saw Colton today ? Was he alone ?" I asked.

"Yes he was alone and he remembered me. I called him to pick you up the other day, remember ? He asked if I knew what happened to you after he left. And he almost cried. You're a lucky bitch man, he still loves you. He just needs some time. I told him you're staying with me. Just as a platonic friend of course."But why didn't he answer my message," I asked Chris. "I'm not supposed to tell you this, but I don't wanna see you suffer more than you already do. He said after you completed your counseling he will get in touch with you. He needs distance from you right now. You hurt and disappointed him a few times even after you promised him you would change," Chris explained.

"But I still have 8 weeks of counseling to do. I can't be without him for 8 weeks," I said and started crying.

I didn't even get horny anymore since Colton broke up with me. Nothing had meaning to me anymore since that night. A few days later I saw Chris coming from the bathroom, pitching a tent in his boxers. I instantly felt a tingling sensation in my cock. He went into his bedroom and left the door cracked open. Theoretical I was single and could fuck around as much as I wanted too. But I wasn't in the mood. Colton was constantly on my mind. One day I drove over to his house and parked across the entrance gate. I waited 3 hours and I actually saw Colton briefly in his car, driving through the gate. I was about to leave, when I saw him coming back out to the street. But he wasn't in his car, he walked straight towards me. I was embarrassed about being caught spying on him. But what the hell, I got to see Colton. He came closer and my heart began to race. I was nervous again like I was the first time I went on a date with him.

"Colton please, talk to me," I said to him. He didn't say anything, he came to the passenger side and got in my car. He was sitting on the passenger seat and looked at me with tears in his eyes. He was holding my hand.

"Colton please, I can do anything you want, but please, I need you. I don't function right without you."

"Kent, I love you more than I ever loved somebody. And I know you feel sorry for your actions but I'm afraid it will happen again if we see each other too soon, before your counseling is done," he told me.

"Can you at least hold me in your arms for a bit babe," I asked. He didn't hesitate one second. He pulled me over to him and held me in his arms for quite a while. It felt so comforting and secure being so close to Colton again. After a while Colton said: "Call me tomorrow and we will go from there." He got out of my car and walked back to the house. I was sitting there for at least another 10 minutes, thinking about Colton until I finally left.

Chris was home when I got there. He was sleeping naked on the couch. I saw fresh cum on his belly and balls. He must've fallen asleep after he jerked off. It kinda turned me on, my dick was getting bigger. I pulled my pants down and went closer to Chris. I stroked my cock right over Chris's cock. My legs were touching the couch and the stroking must've woken him up. I didn't notice when he opened his eyes and watched me beating my meat. I shot my load on his dick and nuts, some sprayed on his belly. His dick was suddenly twitching. With his right hand he wiped mine and his cum off his belly and spread it on his chest. He licked the rest off his fingers.

"I'm gonna let it dry and go to work like that," Chris said. I was kinda embarrassed being caught jerking off on him while he was sleeping. But he thought it was hot.

I was wondering what Colton was doing, I missed him so much. I had to call him, I didn't wanna wait until the next day.

"Hey babe, I wanted to hear your voice again. I'm so glad you talked to me today. I miss you. I wish I could lay next to you in your arms right now," I told him on the phone.

"Yes that would be nice, but it also would be nice if all of this bullshit never would've happened. It takes a while to build trust again but we work on it. Why don't you come over tomorrow for a few," Colton said.

"Sure babe, I love that idea. I was such an idiot and took you for granted. Have a good night. See ya tomorrow."

I told Chris the news about Colton and me. He didn't seem to be glad about it.

"Cool, you can go back to your stud soon, I guess," was all he said. The next morning when I woke up, I saw his bedroom door was cracked open again. I got off the couch and walked over to his door. I looked inside his room and saw him lying on his back. He had his legs spread and worked his asshole with a big fat dildo. "You can come in if you want," he said to me half moaning and half mumbling. Out of a reflex I tried to hide but it was too late anyway. "Don't be shy, we already saw each other naked shooting our jizz," he said.

I went to the bathroom without giving him an answer. I heard him yelling from the bedroom: "Oh I'm not good enough for you, I get it. I'm not a sexy fucker like your Colton." What was his problem, I thought to myself. I took a shower and got ready to go to my counseling appointment and to see Colton afterwards. I felt like the happiest man on earth. The counseling took one hour. When it finally was over I gave Colton a call. "Babe I'm done with my appointment. I'm coming over now. I can't wait to see you."

"Are you sure you wanna see me? Maybe it's not a good idea and we should wait," he said.

"What ? What's the matter ?"

"I just got a call from your roommate Chris. He said he is happy for us and he thinks I'm a cool guy because I don't mind you having sex with him," Colton told me. I almost dropped my phone. My hands were shaking and I panicked, thinking Colton changed his mind because of that two faced, bartending shit eater Chris.

"Babe I promise you I did not have sex with him or anybody else. I kinda spied on him and jerked off but that's it. Now I know why he acted weird earlier today. He wants you to be mad at me, that's why he told you that. He wants to separate us because he has a crush on me. I will tell you everything in person, ok ?"

"Ok, come over," he said. Ten minutes later I was at the house. He opened the door for me, even though I still had my own key. We hugged each other before I went inside.

"It feels so fucking comforting to have you so close to me," I said and almost cried again.

"Same here baby, same here," was Colton's answer. I told him exactly what happened between Chris and me. "You were always on my mind babe, I wasn't even in the mood for sex. I just got caught in the moment when I saw him lying there naked and covered in cum," I said.

"That's ok, I probably would've done the same. I didn't really believe you had sex with him," Colton told me.

"If I see this fucking Chris later today, he better makes his last will, because if I'm done with him, he is dead. I mean the old Kent would've talked like that but the new Kent knows better and learned from his counseling sessions," I corrected myself.

Colton laughed and whispered to me: "I would totally understand if you punched him for his lie."

I took it as Colton's permission. We had no sex that day but we had a good time. It was almost like dating a good friend.

"Can I see you tomorrow ?" I asked Colton.

"Of course babe. I miss you too. You have no idea how hard it was for me to tell you not to come back. But I needed time to think. And I believe we both learned a lesson, not to take anything for granted and how much it hurts to be separated from each other," Colton said to me when he walked me to my car.

When I got back to Chris's place, he wasn't home. There was a big bottle of Vodka on the coffee table. Did he put it there for me ? I told him I don't drink alcohol anymore. I knew what he was trying to do. I took the bottle and poured about one quarter down the drain to make him believe I had a few drinks. He thought if he gets me drunk I would have sex with him or he would tell Colton I'm drinking again. But he had no idea how I get when I drink. He didn't know how mean I could become.

When he came home from work that night, I was already sleeping on the couch. I woke up when I felt something between my legs. It was Chris trying to open my zipper. I got off the couch and punched him twice in his face. As hard as I could. The second punch sent him to the floor. He bled from his nose and chin. He lost one front tooth and his left eye was bruised.

"You fucking little prick, you're lucky I didn't drink the Vodka or you would be dead by now," I yelled at him.

"Why did you lie to Colton, why did you even call him. You wanna be a friend ? But your plan is not working, Colton and I belong together and you can't change that."

He still didn't move or say anything. I got closer to him and saw blood on the side of his head. He must've hit the corner of the table. I was shaking him to wake him up, but he didn't respond. I tried to feel his pulse but I didn't feel anything. I thought I didn't do it right. Then I noticed he didn't breathe. I panicked and didn't know what to do. I finally got the idea and tried CPR on him but had no success. My hands were shaking and my heart was racing. I packed all my stuff including a bottle of Vodka. I erased all evidence about me being there. I deleted Coltons and my number on his phone. I checked all of his text messages. I was hoping he didn't tell anybody about me staying at his place. But in case he did, I would say I moved out earlier that day. I had to make it look like someone broke into his apartment because he was dealing with illicit substances and one deal went bad. I wiped my fingerprints off the key he gave me to his apartment and pressed it on his fingers, so only his fingerprints would be on it. I put the key back in the drawer where Chris had it before he gave it to me. I freaked out even more when I heard the sirens of a cop car driving by. But he didn't stop. I was nauseous and thought I was gonna barf any second.

I thought about what Colton would say when I told him about this. Or shouldn't I tell him ? Should I call him before I make any more decisions or should I just go over to his house ? What if he breaks up with me for good if he knows what I did ? Or if the cops find out about me and I have to go to prison for a very long time. Colton probably wouldn't wait for me that long and would find someone else ? All those questions were going through my mind.

I grabbed all my stuff and left the apartment. I closed the door but didn't lock it because I had to come back for one more important thing to do. I went to my car and called a friend. I told him I needed one or two grams of any illicit street drug he can get. Thirty minutes later I pulled up at my friend's house and picked up what I needed. I went back to Chris's place and made sure nobody saw me. He always reused his ziplock bags so they already had his fingerprints on it. I was wearing gloves, took one of his used ziplock bags and put the drug in it. I hid the bag under his mattress. I left the apartment but that time I locked the door. When I got back to my car I drove off as fast as possible. I just drove around for about twenty minutes. Suddenly I felt lightheaded and I had to pull over. I opened my car door and puked right in front of someone's mailbox. I started to get hot flashes and a panic attack. I cried and couldn't stop. I called Colton, I needed him to pick me up.

"Colton, it's me. Please come and pick me up. I can't drive. I don't even know where I am. I threw up. I did something horrible. Please don't hate me for it, please. I need you right now. I swear, if you don't wanna see me anymore, I kill myself."

"What the hell happened Kent ? Where are you ? Why did you throw up ? You need to calm down babe. I'm here for you, don't worry. Everything will be fine. Where can I find you ? Check your GPS to see where you are babe. I will be there and get you. Don't worry."

I couldn't even look up the address on my GPS where I was. I was too messed up to do anything. I forgot that Colton and I had installed an app on our phones to see each other's location. But he remembered and that's how he found me. His daughter Mercedes came with him to drive my car home. She was just visiting Colton when I called. I got into Colton's car. He was holding me in his arms for a while before we drove home.

"Babe, babe you have to believe me. I'm not a murderer, you know that, right ?" I said to Colton.

"What happened, tell me. Of course you're not a murderer. Why ? Did you. No. Tell me it's not true. You did not, right ?" Colton stuttered.

"He's dead babe, he's fucking dead," I screamed.

"I killed him. I shouldn't be with you, you're too good for me. I'm a murderer babe, you're married to a murderer. But it was an accident. I swear, it was an accident. I just punched him in the face. We can't tell anybody. They won't believe me. Even if they believe it was an accident, I will be locked up for quite a while and that would be the end of us, of us and our marriage. You know that," I said to Colton.

He couldn't say anything for a few minutes. He was just driving. Then he said: "Of course I believe you. I know you're still working on your anger issues but you wouldn't kill somebody. I'm your husband and I will stand on your side in good times and in bad times. Remember ?"

I was so relieved when he said that. It made me feel much better. I told him everything I did at Chris's apartment to hide the fact that I was there.

When we got home, Mercedes left. She had no clue what happened. We went inside the house. Colton took me in his arms and said:

"Welcome home baby. I missed you every minute you were gone. I won't let you go ever again. His bulge in his pants was rubbing against mine, but we both didn't get hard. We were still shocked and too emotional to think about sex.

Two days later we heard on the news, a male body was found dead in his apartment. They also showed a picture. It was Chris. I got goosebumps when I saw it on Tv. They already arrested a suspect, a local drug dealer. Colton and I looked at each other and smiled. "Damn babe, at least something good came out of this," Colton said.

"Yes but Chris is dead because of me. He was a good guy. He didn't deserve to die. It was nothing really bad what he did. Ok, he tried to split us apart and he opened my zipper. But that's no reason to kill someone. Imagine what his parents have to go through now. The same as you would go through if someone would kill me," I said.

Colton had no answer for what I said. That meant I was right.

"I know baby boy, I'm sorry it happened to you and you have to go through this. You probably learned more from this than from five years of counseling," Colton said after a while.

"I wanna make you feel good babe but I still can't concentrate on sex," I said.

"That's ok. I'm really fucking horny though Kent. How about you just open your hot sexy fuckhole for me and I slam my dick inside of you until I cum. I need to unload bad."

"Yes I love to have you inside of me and feel your cock going in and out. Breeding me and making love to me." I suddenly was horny enough just from talking about it. I was naked in a few seconds, so was Colton. He lubed up his finger and probed my hole, twisted and turned it around inside and made me moan. He pulled his finger out and replaced it with his cock.

He buried it balls deep inside my ass and bent down to kiss me and holding my hand while he was fucking me. Every thrust of his pounding cock made my head bang against the headboard. It felt so good to have Colton's cock inside of me again while he was holding my hands and kissing me. It didn't take long though and Colton gave me his seed. I could've let him fuck me like that for hours. He pulled out and with two fingers he stretched my hole open. His cum was dripping out of me. He put his tongue to my asshole and slurped every drop out of me. Then he put his lips on mine and gave me a sloppy, wet cum kiss. I sucked all of his cum into my mouth and swallowed it. I called it a recycled snowball.

"Wow baby boy, I'm feeling much better now," Colton said to me and wiped his dick clean. We went to bed early that night and cuddled up to each other. I held Colton tight in my arm and I had that secure feeling again, Colton always gives me.

It was already 10 am the next morning when we woke up. I had a morning wood and I must've had a wet dream too. Coltons butt hair was sticky on some spots, where my cock head touched his hairy ass when I was sleeping. I slowly got out of bed. I didn't want to, Colton's warm and comforting body felt so good cuddled up against mine. But I had to piss. I went to the bathroom, held my cock over the toilet and pissed. Colton came in too, he had a hard on himself.

He stood next to me and tried to piss.

"I don't think you can piss with that rock hard boner. Be careful you don't piss on the toilet water tank," I said and pushed Colton's boner down with my hand.

"You know what, I have the perfect solution for that," Colton said. He stepped behind me, spread my ass cheeks apart and drilled his rigid morning wood into my fucktube.

"See babe, the angle of my dick is just perfect," he said and flooded my ass with a strong stream of hot morning piss.

"Babe stop, it's too much. When you pull out it will spill on the floor. I can't hold that much," I said.

"Don't worry," he said to me and stuck two fingers next to his dick into my hole. Then he pulled his hard penis out.

"See babe, I plugged you up tight. Now sit down on the toilet and when I pull my fingers out you can let loose."

I sat on the toilet with Colton's fingers inside my ass. Then he pulled them out. I heard the hard, forceful stream coming out of my hole, hitting the toilet water. It was kinda hot, sitting naked on the crapper in front of Colton and shit his piss out of my ass.

"That's my boy," he said and dried his dick off.

My phone was ringing, but I was still shitting Colton's piss out. He answered my phone and told the caller, I will call him back.

He suddenly looked nervous when he said the cops called and needed me to come to the office to answer a few questions.

I called back and asked what this was about. It was about Chris.

"Shit, how did they find out about me? I can't go there Colton. I may not come back if I go."

"You have to go or you make yourself look suspicious. I go with you. And if they arrest you, I bail you out. If they really wanna prosecute you for that, we have to disappear. Very easy," Colton said and tried to calm me down.

"Yes please come with me for moral support. I'm scared baby."

We went to the police office. The officer who called took us to his room.

"Who are you Sir," he asked Colton. "I'm Kent's partner Colton and I'm as curious as he is why he has to appear here today."

"Ok Mr. Colton, you can attend the interview. Would you mind if I ask you a few questions too ?" Colton didn't mind.

"Ok Mr. Colton, did you know Chris Smith ? He worked as a bartender for a local campground. Or you Mr. Kent ?"

Colton answered first. I didn't know what to say. Would it be better to say yes or no ?

Colton said: "I've been at the campground once and had one drink at the bar. I don't know what the bartender's name was and I don't know anybody by that name. My partner Kent was also there once. He told me he had a good conversation with the bartender. I think Kent gave him a ride home that night."

I went along with Colton's story. The officer asked me: "Do you drive a black Daimler-Benz 560 SEC ?"

"Yes I do."

"Neighbors of Mr. Chris Smith reported a car like yours parked at the apartment building frequently. Was it your car and did you and Mr. Smith see each other frequently ?"

I looked at Colton. When he moved his eyes up and down it meant yes and left and right meant no. He looked up and down.

"Yes officer, I saw Mr Smith occasionally," I told him. He asked how long and how often I saw Chris and if I saw him on the day when he died.

Colton asked the officer: "Why do you think Chris got murdered, couldn't it be suicide or an accident ? I heard you arrested a suspect."

"Mr. Smith had several bruises in his face, one on his eye, one on his chin and a broken nose. He also had a hole on the side of his head. I don't think he inflicted all those injuries to himself."

"Yes, that makes sense, officer," Colton said.

The cop told us that he didn't have any more questions and we could go home. I was more than relieved when we left the building.

"See I told you, it's just a routine procedure," Colton said to me.

"I hope so, I almost shit my pants at the police station," I said.

A few days later two cops came to the house again and asked Colton questions about me. But like my husband , he refused to answer them.

"What's going on Colton ? They know something, don't you think ? I'm gonna rot in prison for the rest of my life," I said and panicked. I packed all my stuff in one suitcase. Colton was also worried, I could see it in his eyes.

"Babe, if we disappear everybody thinks you're guilty," Colton mentioned.

"I don't care, they already think so anyway. Please Colton, let us go somewhere where we can start over again and nobody can find us," I begged.

It wouldn't be easy and we had to act fast. We both knew there was something the cops didn't tell us. Colton checked the Sheriff's website and suddenly yelled at me:

"Kent, they have a warrant out for your arrest. And for me too as an accomplice. Are they fucking crazy ?"

Colton also packed one suitcase with his stuff. We went to the bank to get enough money for our trip. But the accounts were already frozen.

"Fucking bull crap shit, what we gonna do now," I asked.

Colton quitclaimed everything he had to his daughter. We put our stuff in the Mercedes and left town an hour later. We had only $ 2000, Colton's cash emergency fund he always was hiding in the couch. But what would we do if the money's gone ?

"My daughter can send us more cash when we need it. The cops can't keep the accounts frozen when the quitclaim is through.

For the moment we had enough $ for gas to get to Argentina. We were on the road for ten days when we finally arrived in Buenos Aires. Our money went for gas, food and motel rooms. We could sell the car but I wasn't crazy about the idea. Colton couldn't get a hold of his daughter to tell her about sending us money in a way that wasn't traceable. But there was no untraceable way.

Colton risked everything he had, when he signed it over to his daughter. All because of me. But we still had each other. That was more important than anything else. We started to sleep in our car.

"Colton, what are we gonna do without money in a strange country ?" I asked him.

"We get a job or we sell your ass. Always think positive baby boy, everything is better than being in prison. We are still together, that's what counts. If we hadn't left home we would be incarcerated right now. And we wouldn't be together in one cell."

We had about $ 100 left. Enough to eat and drive around to look for a job. But we didn't find one. We didn't speak the language and had no work permit. We bought bread, cheese and milk for dinner. We were sitting on the back seat in our car and ate the few things we had. We locked the doors and snuggled up in the back seat. The windows were tinted dark enough, so nobody could see us.

It didn't take long and we fell asleep in each other's arms. The daylight of the next day woke us up.

"Hey, let's go fishing. Fish, lobster, whatever we catch we can sell," Colton suggested. We drove south of Buenos Aires to La Plata, a small laid back town. We spent all day at the beach and by late afternoon we had caught enough fish to sell. We went to the town's market and got 500 Pesos for them, which is about $ 30.- We went back to the beach and built a fire pit. We started a fire to cook a few fish we saved for us.

"We actually had a nice day, don't you think Colton ?"

"Yes I liked it too, and it beats being in prison."

We bought a few beers and after a while we were tired enough to fall asleep on the sandy beach.

I missed having sex, it's kinda cramped in the back of a car but we will manage it somehow. Colton called a friend of ours back home today. He told him to let his daughter Mercedes know what happened and that we needed money badly. He told our friend Jeff:"Tell Mercedes I call her on Buffies phone tomorrow at 5 pm your time."

Everything worked out. Mercedes picked up Buffies phone when Colton called her. Nobody else knew who Buffie was, just in case the cops tapped her phone.

"Hey Dad, you're a criminal and fugitive now. That's so cool. You and Kent were on the news yesterday. They think you're probably in a different state. Where are you by the way ?" she was babbling. "I can't tell you right now over the phone but you have to send money as soon as possible. I just don't know how to do it, so the cops can't trace us. We need at least one million dollars. I will call you again in two days," Colton explained to her.

"Until we get the money, we have to go fishing a few more times I guess," I said to Colton and gave him a kiss.

"Or we have to sell your cute little butt," Colton joked.

Colton had an idea. He told Mercedes about it, when he called her two days later. She was supposed to give someone she trusts the money in a sealed envelope. That person would meet us somewhere around the airport in Buenos Aires.

When we had the cash, we wanted to go to Brazil and buy a small house for us.

Everything worked out great. Four days later we drove to Buenos Aires. We met up with the guy at the airport. We went to McDonalds with him so it wouldn't look suspicious. We had something to eat and Colton took the envelope from the guy. He opened it to check if the cash was still in it. It was exactly $ 945,000.-

We took off one hour later, Brazil as our destination.

Brazil was nice, I liked it but we were not used to the lifestyle. I missed Florida and our home. Colton felt the same way.

We rented a nice little house in the suburbs of Rio de Janeiro.

"At least we get around and see south america," I said to Colton.

"Yeah, it would be nicer if we were here just on vacation. I'm kinda homesick babe. I was thinking, instead of blowing the money here on rent or whatever, I can buy the best attorney in the U.S. and maybe we can go back home if he can help us. It should be easy to prove that I'm not an accomplice and you can maybe get away with a few months in jail or so. What do you think about it ?" he asked me.

"Well it can't hurt trying but what if he can't work out a deal with the prosecutor and help me ? Until I know for sure I would rather stay here babe," I said.

"Ok, I'm gonna go online to find the best attorney. After I talked to one, we will know more and can decide what we do. Sounds good ?"

"Yeah, sounds like a plan. What would I do without you," I said to Colton.

It took Colton almost two days to find a lawyer he thought would be worth the money. He asked for a flat rate of $ 650,000.-

He told Colton his success rate is 95 %.

Colton hired him and told Mercedes to pay for the lawyer.

Only three days later our attorney Jan Sorensen came to visit us in Rio de Janeiro.

"Wow, he is even flying to Brazil to visit his clients. I guess you get what you pay for," I said to Colton.

We had an appointment with him at 2 pm at our house. We saw him from the window getting out of the cab.

"Holy fuckn cow. This hunk is a lawyer ? He must have huge bull balls the way his pants is bulging out," I said more to myself than to Colton.

I opened the door and let him in.

"Jan Sorensen, nice to meet you," he introduced himself and shaked my hand. His hand felt soft and warm, his palm was damp from sweating. He looked into my eyes, when he talked.

"Hello, I'm Kent Sabel and this is Colton. I hope you can help us to get back home to Florida. Where are you from ?"

"I'm not far from you. I live in Miami but I also have a vacation home here in Brazil. You guys are welcome to stay there until you go back to Florida."

"If we can go back," Colton interrupted.

"Hi. You must be the brother Colton," Jan asked.

"No, actually we are married and Kent is my husband," Colton corrected him.

"That's great. You guys are married. I'm still looking for the right partner," he said. Did he admit that he is gay ? I had to check out that huge bulge between his legs. I tried not to stare at it but he caught me anyway. He just smiled. "I'm also gay by the way," he said.

"I figured when I saw you at the door," I said.

"Aw, is that a good thing or bad," he asked me.

"Good of course, for me at least. I mean for other people too, I guess. Well what I meant was, I don't know what I'm saying. I'm just babbling. I better shut up now," I said and Colton agreed. He noticed that there was a spark between Jan and me. We talked about our case for over two hours. He told us again, when he was leaving, he would be glad to have us as his guests in his house until he goes back to Miami.

Colton didn't like the idea. That was the first time he showed signs of jealousy since I knew him. I asked Jan if I could give him a ride to his house but he got Colton's hint and said no.

After he left, Colton actually got upset. "I can't believe this, I'm paying this guy $ 650,000 and he is flirting with my husband," Colton said.

"Since when do you get jealous ? You don't really think I and Jan would do such a nasty thing."

"No, but still. Now I know how jealousy feels," Colton said.

"Hey babe, if his crush on me helps us to win our case, let him."

"Yeah I know. But he gets paid to win, not to have a crush on his clientele."

"But I think we should go and visit him at least once as long as he is still here. It can only help," I said.

"Ok. We visit him and have a wild sex orgy. That would help even more, don't you think ?" Colton said and grinned.

Jan stayed at his house for another three days before he was heading back to Miami. I called him the night before we were planning to visit him.

"Hi Jan, it's Kent. Colton and I thought we would stop by your house before you have to leave, if that's ok."

"Absolutely, yes come over and we have a couple drinks at the pool," he responded.

The next day we drove to Jan's house. It was located about twenty minutes from ours.

When he opened the door he was wearing only tight shorts.

He's really showing off his assets, I thought to myself. His bulge was bigger than I had imagined. I couldn't get my hand around it, if I wanted to.

He made some cocktails for us before we went to the pool. I couldn't help myself, but the pure sight of his manhood bulging out his swimsuit made my dick grow. I tried to fight it, but the more I thought about stopping my erection, the bigger it got. I turned around so my dick would face the pool wall but Colton and Jan saw me pressing my hard drill against the concrete wall.

"You don't need to be embarrassed, it happens to me every time I see a good looking guy. It probably will happen soon to myself," Jan said to me. I looked over to Colton, he definitely looked mad.

I tried to change the subject and we talked about mine and Colton's court case. He had no doubt that Colton won't be sentenced at all and I could face a maximum sentence of probably six month,maybe just probation.

"Probation ? Even I'm responsible for somebody's death ?" I asked.

"Yeah, I have my connections and ways to get what I'm shooting for," Jan answered.

"I'm sure you do," Colton mumbled.

"So you guys don't worry, when you call me and I tell you it's safe to come back to Florida, you just come back like nothing happened," Jan said to us but looked at me.

Colton gave me a sign, he wanted to leave.

Damn,I thought. I wanted Jans big cock. Usually I was the jealous one and now I wanted another guys cock up my ass and Colton was jealous.

"Ok Jan, we gotta run. We call you about once or twice a week to see what's new," I told him. We shaked hands and Colton and I left. Before we went home, we walked around in Rio, looking at all those pretty brazilian boys. Colton didn't say much, he was still upset about Jan Sorensen. He saw him as a threat.

"Babe," I said, "you don't need to be upset about this lawyer guy. He can do or say what he wants, I love you and I will always remember the vows we exchanged. I would never cheat or leave you for anybody else. We already went through so much shit together, how could I give up on you for someone else." Colton believed me and it made him feel better. "Come on, let's try some Brazilian ice cream," he said. We bought a half gallon of Coconut - Mango ice cream, went to the beach and watched the sunset.

"Let's get a bottle of Rum or something and get drunk," Colton said. I never heard him saying he wants to get drunk until now. I knew why. We both missed our home and Florida. He was in that situation just because of me.

"Oh no, never mind," he corrected himself. He remembered the alcohol problem I had. After sunset we drove back to our house and went to bed. We both fell asleep depressed that night.

The week passed by without anything exciting. Except one day we checked out a local sex shop.

I said to Colton: "Why don't we check out a brazilian sex shop ? It's probably packed with hot Brazilian guys." Colton liked the idea. It was something to do and we both were horny anyway. We found one in the center of Rio and even got a parking spot right in front of it. We walked inside but it was just a store with a few toys and magazines.

"It looks like one of our sex shops back in the fifties," Colton said. The man behind the register asked us in english: "Can I help you ? Do you look for something specific ?" Colton told him we were looking for a theater or a private booth. The cashier smiled and told us to follow him outside. There was an entrance at the side of the building which led downstairs to the basement. "Where is he going with us? It's creepy down here," I said. There was another steel door. The guy opened it and we stepped into a perfectly equipped playroom. There were at least ten men fucking and sucking each other. There were three slings, a maze with glory holes, a big rubber mattress on the floor and a big screen tv playing porn. At the right side of the play room were five private rooms. Colton and I took our cocks out and watched the guys fucking and playing.

I was getting hard and had to stroke my cock. There was a hairy man tied to a wooden cross. Another guy said to a muscled stud handling a whip :

"Hit his fucking cock head with the whip and make him scream. I wanna know if it makes him hard."

He hit the poor hairy guy's cock head hard with the first hit. The hairy bear screamed loud when the whip plowed down on his head. With the second and third hit his cock got actually harder and he started to pump out a big load of jizz that splashed in all directions with each hit of the whip. By then five men were standing around watching and stroking their cocks. The bear was done and I went over to the sling area. To get there I had to pass a bathtub where one guy was sitting inside of it and three other guys were standing around and pissed on him. He tried to get as much piss in his mouth as possible. The sling action seemed more interesting to me. One guy was lying in a sling and got fucked hard. In the other sling a skinny guy got fisted by a tall muscled man with tattoos on his arms and legs. He had his right arm almost to the elbow inside the guy's rectum. It seemed like they both were really into it. The man that got fisted was moaning and his cock was hard as a rock. Every time the tattooed guy moved his hand inside of his ass, his dick jerked and precum was oozing out of his piss slit. I wouldn't mind feeling that cock inside of me. One hot little fucker climbed on top of him, grabbed his cock and when he felt his fat purple head on his hole, he lowered himself down until the eighth inches disappeared in his ass. His precum was the perfect lube. He was riding the skinny man's cock hard and the muscled guy gave him a good prostate massage from the inside. The poor guy couldn't hold back his cum any longer and seeded the little guy's fucktube with his massive hot load. I stepped closer and stroked my cock as fast as I could, pulled my foreskin back and fore until I exploded on his stomach. The tattooed guy pulled his arm out of his ass and slammed his dick inside, followed by his fist again. It took him only a few plows and he jizzed deep inside. The guy riding on the fisted guy still had his cock inside of him and could feel another load filling him up even more. He raised his ass up until the fisted man's fat dick slapped on his belly. Two cum loads leaked out of the little guy's freshly fucked hole and dripped on the fisted guys nut sack, running down to his ass and coated the tattooed guys cock. "Thank's guys, that was fucking hot," I said to them both. Colton was standing next to me, when he got close to shoot his seed shortly after I unloaded. I kneeled down in front of Colton and waited for him to blast his cum. When he felt his semen rising up inside his fuck pole, he put his dick head on my lips and sprayed his white gold on my tongue. I swallowed my man's gooey, stringy nut juice.

"Damn babe that was fucking hot shit. See, we can have fun just by watching others and stroke off together," I said to Colton.

"I never said we can't. I just like a three way sometimes but I respect your jealousy and don't even ask for it," Colton said and grinned.

"Let's get out of here, I don't even know if this is legal in Brazil, what we're doing here," I whispered.

"Probably not, or why do you think we're doing this in a hidden basement," Colton answered. We went back upstairs and opened the door to the street. Nobody was there so we got outside and walked to our car. When we came home Colton thought about calling Jan Sorensen our lawyer.

"Yeah, call him. It can't hurt to ask what he did for us so far," I said. Colton called him but forgot about the time difference between Brazil and Florida. Jan was already home.

"Damn it. He's not in his office any more. But I don't wanna call him at home. Can you call him since he is your little lover boy who has a crush on you ?" Colton joked.

"Sure thing," I said and dialed the number.

Jan answered his phone. "Hello Kent, what a nice surprise in the early evening. I was actually just thinking about you a little while ago. I don't have a charming and handsome man like you every day as a client."

Colton heard what Jan said and held his middle finger up in my direction and smiled.

I returned the compliment just to make brownie points for our benefit.

"Oh you're making me blush Jan. And I don't have a hung, sexy man like you every day as an attorney.I'm really flattered that you think I'm charming and handsome. But I think my husband is better looking than I am. So, what have you done for us so far? You don't wanna see your charming and handsome client behind bars. "

Colton gave me a thumbs up. "Well I talked to the district attorney and to the prosecutor. They owe me a few if you know what I mean. I also talked to a few friends, one of them is a judge and coincidentally he will be the judge that is handling your and your husband's case."

"Wow, that was quick. You're, you're, I don't know what to say," I said.

"I'm awesome, I know. It was a pleasure to help you. Maybe down the road I need your help and I will gladly accept it. We just have to wait for a court date. As soon as I know it I let you know right away so you guys can be here on time."

"Ok, thanks again Jan. We will see you in a few weeks I guess," I said and hung up. "Did you hear that baby ? In a few weeks we can be back home," I said to Colton who was also very excited.

We were debating if we should stay at our rental until Jan would call us with the court date or if we already should drive to Mexico. From there it wouldn't be such a long way to Florida than from Brazil, in case we had only a few days' notice before the court date. We decided to go to Mexico, somewhere close to the Texas borderline and wait there for our court date.

The next day we spent packing our few things and put them in our car. We went one last time to the beach where we spent so many evenings, watching the sunset. At that point we even liked it there, we saw everything from a different point of view because we knew we could go home soon. Suddenly it felt more like being on vacation.

We left Rio de Janeiro on the next day around 10 am. We drove about 6 to 7 hours every day. When we finally arrived at the Mexican border, the Check Engine light came on.

"Fuckn bullshit. Why is that damn light on ? The car has only 28,000 miles," I yelled more to myself than to Colton.

"It could be a reminder for the next inspection babe," Colton said.

"Or something more serious," I answered, when the engine stalled out. We were stuck somewhere in the Guatemalan desert but only about five miles south of the border to Mexico. Colton tried to get the number of any business with a tow truck. After about thirty minutes he finally got a number and called. The truck was supposed to arrive in about one hour.

"Let's play 'The car mechanic and his stranded daddy.' I'm the mechanic and you're the daddy whose car broke down and is trying to fix it. You bend over to check if you have enough fuel. And there comes the mechanic, steps behind you, opens his zipper, pulls your pants down and puts his fuel injector hose inside your tank opening. After he injected his high octane grade fuel into your fuel hungry tank, your fuel pump starts to deliver and your injector sprays it all over the hot engine," I suggested to Colton.

"It should be the opposite. Since when do you fill up my tank, huh ? How about you are the escaped prison bitch and I'm the guard and I caught you in the dessert and fuck you right there as your punishment," Colton said and grinned.

"We can play both role plays if we have enough time," I said.

"Come over here prison bitch, you get fucked inside the car right this second," Colton ordered. But we didn't have time to play. The tow truck arrived fifteen minutes after Colton called instead of one hour later. How could they miscalculate the arrival time by forty five minutes ? But I didn't complain. We got towed to the next available repair shop. The mechanic told us he would look at it in the morning. There was a small motel across the street where we stayed over night.

"What room number do you guys have ? I come over and knock as soon as I know what's wrong with your vehicle," the mechanic said.

I told him Room 104. There was even a phone and tv in our room but the tv didn't work. "We have to entertain each other I guess with the tv not working," I said to Colton and put my hand between his hairy legs. "Not now you horny little brat. I need to call Jan before it gets too late," Colton responded.

"Yeah, call Jan. Tell him I miss him. He didn't call me brat, he called me a charming, handsome man, remember ?" I joked with Colton.

"Yeah, yeah. Whatever. He doesn't have to put up with you every day, brat," Colton joked back.

He called Jan to find out if there was anything new. Jan answered the phone and thought it was me calling, when he saw the country code from Guatemala on his caller ID. This time he got even bolder.

"Hello Mr. sexy man. I was waiting for your call to hear your seductive voice again."

"Hello Mr. Sorensen. I didn't know you are thinking I'm a sexy man," Colton said and played dumb. "Oh, is this Colton ? I'm so sorry. I was expecting someone else's phone call and we always joke around," Jan explained.

"That's ok. Anything new ?" Colton asked him.

"Yes. I got the court date just two hours ago. It's Monday June 13th. 9 am. That's in about four weeks. Or no, actually it's in three and a half weeks," Jan said.

"Ok, we will be there Mr. Sorensen," Colton said and hung up.

"Did you hear it Kent ? We have to hang out here for three more weeks. Or we just go back home and if we get arrested before the court date we could bail ourselves out."

"Going home sounds better," I answered.

I pulled the bed sheets off the bed and layed down. Colton stripped his clothes off and took a shower. I need one too, I thought and followed Colton. "Wait, I soap up your back," I said and jumped in the shower.

"What happened to the escaped prison bitch ?" I asked Colton. "Aw that one. Yeah well, I had mercy on her and let her go. But she followed me to the shower and is soaping up my back right now."

"You had mercy on her ? She didn't wanna have mercy, she wants to be punished, she is really bad," I joked. I put a lot of body wash on my hand and soaped up Colton's back, running my hand down to his ass crack and made sure the foam covered every inch between his butt cheeks. I circled my finger around his fuckhole muscle and felt it twitching from the stimulation I applied. The sight of his wet black butt hair and his tanned ass cheeks made my dick rise. My hand moved lower, leaving Colton's shithole and slid between his sexy tattooed legs. Then my soapy hand played with his nuts and pulled them down until Colton asked me to stop. His cock was jerking and getting bigger in anticipation of what I may do next to him. Colton grabbed my hard pipe and pulled the foreskin back until it was hurting.

"Bad, bad prison bitch," he said and got behind me. He took a hold of my

hips and with one swift thrust he was inside me. He didn't even lube up. I let out a soft scream. "Shut up bitch, it's supposed to hurt," Colton said.

"Yeah punish me you mean, strong prison guard," I said as good as I could, trying to catch my breath. And Colton kept punishing me like there is no tomorrow. "Good strong prison guard, yeah make me sore," I mumbled and turned him on even more. Colton kept holding me by my hip with his left hand and with his right hand he began stroking my cock. He pumped his dick in and out of me until he flooded my inside with his hot sperm. I shot my cum against the shower wall. Colton wiped it off with his finger before it ran down to the tub and made me clean his finger.

"We had almost the same shower breeding session the first day we met on Father's Day last year, remember ?" I asked Colton. "Of course I remember. How could I forget? Soon we have our first anniversary," he answered.

"Yes we have to celebrate that. It's on the 19th this year. One week after our court appearance. We can celebrate our anniversary and to be back home and not in prison," I said.

We laid on the bed and tried to sleep. In the middle of the night I woke up because I felt something on my foot. I looked at my feet and saw a big roach crawling on my toes. I jumped up and screamed like a little girl. Colton woke up from me screaming. He saw the roach and laughed. "Aw, are you scared of a little bug ?" he asked and hit the roach with his bare hand. "That's disgusting, you better make sure to wash your hand a few times before you touch me or my dick again," I told him. I couldn't sleep for the rest of the night, thinking there were more roaches.

It wasn't until 10 am, when the mechanic knocked at our door. "Good news," he said, " it's already fixed. It was only a sensor that malfunctioned and shut the ignition system off."

We went over to his shop and paid for the repair. One hour later we were back on the road. We drove all day, stopped here and there for a break and before it got dark we were at the border to Texas.

"Before we enter Texas I wanna call our lawyer again and tell him we're back in the U.S. and to bail us out if something should go wrong," Colton said to me. He called Jan and told him we would be back in Florida in two days. Everything was fine Jan said and we don't have to worry about anything. We stayed in a Motel in Mexico that night.

"Hey Colton, do you need your back soaped up again tonight ?"

"No, I'm too tired to even get a hard on. I'm laying down and watch Tv until I fall asleep," he answered.

"Well we see about that. The mechanic didn't help the poor stranded daddy yet. You punished only the escaped prison bitch," I joked. He watched Tv and I tried hard to get him. "Babe," he said, "not tonight, please."

"Why, you want me to sit on it ?"

"No. I just told you why."

I sucked his dick anyway but he fell asleep on me. I snuggled up to Colton and fell asleep myself.

At 6 am Colton woke me up. "Get up, we need to get back on the road."

"Let me sleep, I'm still tired."

"Well you should've listened to me last night and not played with my privates. Now get up or I piss on your ear," was Colton's answer.

"In my ear ? That's sick. You're a sick pup. But you can pee in my ass if you want."

"I know but I don't want to. Now get up. We're leaving in 15 minutes."

I had to get up or he would be a real pain in my ass. Not the good kind of pain I liked though.

We left the Motel at 6.40 am and entered Texas twenty minutes later. "Woohoo ! We're back home," I shouted. After we passed the border, I layed down on the back seat and took a power nap. Colton drove for twelve hours straight, when he finally stopped.

"Hey brat, it's your turn driving. We can make it home tonight. But now I need a nap," he said. I got behind the wheel and continued to drive on I-10. We were close to the Florida border.

"In six hours we will be in our own bed again babe," I said but Colton was sleeping and didn't hear me. He did not wake up until I drove through our gate. I parked my car in the garage.

"Good morning Sir. It's about time you wake up," I said to him.

"Why, where are we ?"

"In our garage. After driving 24,000 miles we are back home babe."

"Great. I'm never gonna leave again," Colton said.

I felt the same way.

We went inside the house. Everything was the same way as when we left. It looked like Mercedes wasn't in the house at all. Colton sent her a text to let her know we're back. We had to air out the house before turning the A/C back on. I turned the lights in and around the pool on to see how the water looked. It wasn't too bad. It was green from algae. I shocked the pool with a high dose of chlorine and turned the filter pump and the waterfall pump on. Every two hours I backwashed the filter while I scrubbed the pool walls in the meantime. When the sun came up I started to cut the grass around the house and pool area. Colton cleaned the house inside and did laundry. I also had to wash my car and clean it inside. After living in it for a while and driving for so many hours it was a mess. But when I was done it looked like new again. Maybe Colton buys me a new one for our anniversary, I thought. It was almost one year old and had 31,000 miles on it. Being with Colton I became a spoiled brat. My last car I had before I met Colton was 14 years old and had 240,000 miles on it.

In the afternoon the pool water was clear enough to go in for a swim.

"Come on babe. Let's enjoy our home and relax in the pool with me," I said to Colton.

"I never even asked you. Do you have a nickname ?" I asked him.

"Yeah kinda. In school and College they called me Colt."

"Aw because of your size down there ?"

"Yep. Jealous ?" he asked.

"Nah, I'm happy with what I got."

"What ? How can you be happy with that little dick," Colton joked. I hope he was joking.

"Well at least I'm uncut. Come on, let's get naked and go in the pool. If you behave you can play with my foreskin," I suggested.

"I don't wanna play with your foreskin. Your dick is too small for my standards," he said and grinned. He pulled me close to him and kissed me long and passionately. My dick always gets hard from kissing so Colton wasn't surprised when my dick was hard and poked him between his legs. "Pig," he said and looked down at my cock.

"Yeah, that little pig down there loves you so much it gets hard every time you touch me," I told him.

It was later at night after we enjoyed the pool together and went back inside the house, when Jan Sorensen called.

"What does he want," Colton said and made a face that showed me his disgust for the man.

"Well, answer the phone and you will know."

He didn't wanna talk to Jan and I could understand why, being a jealous person myself. But I was afraid if I talk to him Colton gets even more upset. I answered the phone anyway. "Hey Jan, how's it going ?"

"Good and self ? I'm glad you made it home safe and I could help you to come home again. Listen, I was thinking I should come over to your place and we can hang out for a while and talk before you have to go to your court date. And to be honest, I wanna see you badly. I think I fell in love with you."

That almost made me choke on my own spit.

"Oh, well I'm glad to hear that. I mean, no. That changes a lot. You really think it's a good idea to come over here ?" I asked.

"Please, one last time. I can't sleep or eat. I constantly have to think about you. I know you're married to this guy. I'm sorry but I had to get this off my chest."

"Ok. Can you come tomorrow and we can talk ?" I asked him. He said yes. I was feeling bad for him because I knew how he felt. It happened to me more than once before. I wanted to talk to Jan without

Colton hearing the conversation. I texted him right after we talked on the phone.

"Jan, I know how you must feel. I think we both could have a future together under different circumstances but I married Colton because I love him. I would never cheat on him or leave him for somebody else. I don't mind being friends with you though. I know it would be hard for you. Colton wouldn't appreciate it either. Time will heal and you will get over me and find a great man who loves you. I like you as a person and I will always be thankful for what you did for me and Colton. I wanted you to know this before you come over. Have a good night. See ya tomorrow."

I was honestly nervous about Jan coming over. I didn't know if I should tell Colton about Jan's love for me or not. I didn't wanna hurt anybody's feelings.

"What did he have to say ?" Colton asked.

"He is coming over tomorrow to talk one last time before our court date."

"Oh well. Good for him," was all Colton said.

It was the first night we both slept together in our own bed again. We went to bed very early that night. I think it was around 7 pm.

We were tired and fell asleep right away because we both didn't sleep the night before. I was thinking about Jan. Did he sleep or was he awake all night thinking about me ? It scared me that I was thinking about him too.

At 1 pm Jan showed up the next day. I opened the door for him and let him in. Colton wasn't home. He was running a few errands. We didn't expect Jan that early. I was afraid if Colton came back and Jan was still there it would look like I told Jan to come over while Colton was still out. I went with Jan to the pool. We were sitting at the table so it wouldn't be awkward or suspicious for Colton when he came back.

"I'm glad I can be alone with you before your husband comes home. I totally understand your feelings and I thank you so much for your kind words in your text message last night. I can't forget you but unfortunately I have to get over you. But you will always have a place in my heart if you need me or things go wrong with you and Colton." I almost cried when he talked and he noticed it. We both hugged each other tight and he kissed me on my lips.

"Thank you again for everything you did for me and Colton. I leave it up to you if you wanna stay in touch as a friend or not. It probably makes it harder for you to get over me if you keep seeing me," I told him. He stopped hugging me and was about to leave, when Colton came home.

"Oh Mr. Sorensen. You're gonna leave already ? I'm so sorry I couldn't be here sooner," Colton said in a sarcastic tone.

Jan didn't respond to Colton's comment. For one last time he looked into my eyes and left.

"What's wrong with him ?" Colton asked. "He has some problems and feels depressed," I answered.

"And he comes to you to talk about it ? What's going on Kent ?"

"No he didn't talk about it. He just mentioned it. I don't know what his problems are."

I felt so bad lying to Colton. If I was honest to myself I had to admit that I also had feelings for Jan. But how could that happen ? I loved Colton.

"Ok. So did you talk about our court case ?" Colton asked.

"Yes. I mean no. Colton, please I don't wanna talk about it now." I went inside the house and watched Tv. Colton had a feeling that it had something to do with Jan and me. I could feel that he was worried. I had to talk to him.

"Babe, I need to talk to you. Come sit over here next to me."

"Ohoh. That usually doesn't mean anything good," he said.

"But not necessarily bad either. Jan told me he is in love with me."

"And, are you in love with him too ?" he asked me.

"No. I mean I feel bad for him. I didn't want you to worry that's why I didn't say anything."

"I appreciate what you told me. Honesty is always the best way and remember what we said when we repeated the vows. This love will be your only love."

"I know babe, I know. I just feel sorry for him because I know how it feels when you love somebody but you know there is no future. But this time I'm the one who had to turn someone down. Believe me, it doesn't feel much better than being turned down."

"You're such a good hearted person Kent. I know what you mean. It probably happens to everybody. I love you so much," Colton said.

I didn't see or hear from Jan until our court date. He was sitting in the first row with all the other lawyers. We found a seat in the second row. I was almost sitting behind Jan. I could smell his aftershave. He took a glance at me and I gave him a smile. Colton and I were called to the bench. The judge didn't waste much time or words.

"Mr. Kent Sabel, I found you not guilty for the homicide of Chris Smith. Mr. Colton Sabel, I found you not guilty for being an accomplice in the case of Chris Smith."

"That's it babe. We are free and can go home," I said to Colton. Jan came to my mind again. Without him we would still be in Brazil. When we left the courtroom I turned around to see Jan one last time. He turned his head at the same moment and I saw his sad eyes.

"We should at least say thank you to Jan," I said to Colton. He agreed and we waited outside the building for Jan to come out.

"Where is he?" I asked.

"He's probably fucking the judge right now to thank him. I mean he got a lot of money from us. Maybe he splits the cash with the judge. That's why his success rate is so high and he can ask for those outrageous amounts," Colton said. I didn't believe it. I thought Jan was a good guy. But Colton could've been right. Even a good guy has to make money. I saw him coming out about five minutes later. He stopped when he saw us standing at the door but then continued to walk slowly towards the door. I waved to let him know we're waiting for him.

"See babe, he's not fucking the judge," I said. "Hey Jan. You did a great job. Thank you so much," I said.

"You are very welcome. It was a pleasure to meet you guys. One last thing. I don't wanna take your money. I will send you a check for the full amount you paid me." He walked away without saying anything else. I stood there and became more fascinated with this man. Even his name Jan Sorensen sounded attractive to me. Colton didn't know what to think about him. He was skeptical about Jan. I saw Jan getting in his car and leaving. I couldn't stop thinking about this man during the next couple of days.

Three days later I got mail without the sender's name and address. It was from Jan. In the envelope was a check for $ 650,000 and a note.

"Dear Kent,

When you get this note I will be gone. I can't stop thinking about you. I don't wanna find somebody else, I wanted you. I never felt this way about somebody. Enjoy the money with your husband, I don't need it.

I love you

Jan Sorensen"

I felt my throat getting tight and I had tears running down my cheeks. What did he mean by he will be gone. Where did he go ? He didn't do anything stupid hopefully. I had to find out. I wiped the tears off my face. I went outside to Colton and gave him the check.

"Here babe, Jans check just came in the mail."

"Wow he really sent the money back ? I still can't believe it," Colton said.

"Yep, he did. Oh by the way, I have to go to my parents house. Do you need anything from the store since I'm out ?" I asked Colton. "No, I'm good."

I got dressed and left. I went to Jan's office to find out where he is. His secretary told me he's leaving for Brazil in a few hours but he is still in his office if I need to see him. "Actually yes, I need to talk to him. I know where his office is," I said to her. I opened Jans door without knocking. He was standing at the window and looked outside. When he heard the door, he turned around. He wasn't sure how to respond when he saw me standing there.

"Jan, I'm glad I found you before you leave. Please stay. You don't have to leave. I do have more feelings for you than I told you. I couldn't stop thinking about you. I don't know what to do. I love Colton and our marriage means a lot to me." I stepped closer to Jan.

"That's why I have to leave for a while. I don't wanna be the reason for you and Colton to break up. But I'm really glad you stopped by. I will get over it, I just need some alone time. You should go now, it makes it just harder for me the longer you're here," he said to me.

I was about to leave but I didn't want to. I hugged Jan and kissed him on his lips. He opened his mouth and his tongue entered my mouth. He grabbed my ass and slapped it with one hand. He started breathing harder, our kiss got more intense and passionate. My hands moved down his back and inside his pants. For the first time I could feel his bare ass. He started moaning while I was fingering his hole. We stopped kissing, my lips were wet from his spit. He pulled my shirt over my head. He licked my nipples, then he ran his tongue down my treasure trail. I shivered and my hard cock was already trying to get out of my pants. I looked at the bulging spot between his legs and saw the outline of his rigid penis. We both ripped our pants off. For the first time we both stood naked in front of each other and our hard cocks pointed at each other. Jan pushed his index finger between my foreskin and my dick head. He circled it around the head and made me leak precum. He pulled my foreskin back and took a deep whiff of my head. He licked the precum off my tip . "If I had known you're uncut, I would've raped you a long time ago," Jan said and smiled at me. He turned me around by my hips and spread my ass cheeks with both of his hands. His tongue circled around my hole, making it wet and slippery, ready to take his throbbing cock. He got off his knees and I felt the tip of his head touching my hole. He pulled me back against him and his cock disappeared completely, balls deep inside my tight, man milking fuckhole. I saw colorful stars and circles when he rammed his fat cock all the way in. My stomach felt like it was charged with electricity.

"I don't want this to end," he moaned but his seed was already entering my fuck tube, inseminating me deep. When he was done, he pulled out of me and sucked my cock until I rewarded him with my cum, shooting it down his throat and directly in his stomach.

He was shaking when he got off his knees, his eyes reflected his feelings for me and made them visible.

"Fuck, now what," Jan said. "You made me feel like nobody else before," he said.

Didn't I say the same things to Colton when I met him ? I couldn't believe what I just did. I cheated on Colton for the first time.

"It can't happen again," I told Jan.

"I know. It just happened because we both wanted it. But don't go crazy over it. It doesn't mean you don't love Colton. Everybody is capable of loving more than one person," he said.

"Oh yeah, you think so ? I mean I love Colton but I could imagine falling for you too. You're right. I never thought about it this way. Colton always liked threesomes. Maybe we three could have fun together."

"Well I don't think he wants a three way with me," Jan said.

"Probably not. But I got to go. Are we staying in touch or not ?" I asked.

"I don't know. Let me think about it, Kent. It's probably better if we don't."

I walked back to my car. I felt horrible. I cheated on Colton and I couldn't get Jan off my mind. On my way home I stopped at a flower shop. I bought Colton's favorite flowers, yellow and red orchids. When I came home I gave him the flowers and said: "I'm so sorry babe." I went to the bathroom and took a shower to wash Jans odor off my body.

"Sorry for what," Colton asked. He followed me to the bathroom and grabbed my balls. "What did you do ? Whatever it is, it can't be bad enough for me to rip your nuts off."

"I'm an asshole babe."

"I know but I love that asshole," he said.

I took a towel and dried myself off. "I love you Colton. I made a big mistake. I'm just a male human. You know what I mean ?"

"No, not really."

"I don't know how to tell you babe."

"It can't be that bad. It's not like you had sex with Jan," Colton said and laughed.

"Well. I kinda did."

"What do you mean ? Kinda."

He didn't laugh any more. He fucked you ? Was it good at least ?" Colton was yelling at me.

"It just happened. I didn't want it to happen. I was thinking with my dick head. It won't happen again, I swear."

"At least you told me instead of doing it behind my back. It doesn't make it better but I believe you really feel bad about it," Colton said in his normal calming voice again. "When I think about it, you sold your ass and earned us the $ 650,000 back I gave Jan."

"Yeah I'm not cheap. I'm a high class bitch. So you're not mad at me ?" I asked.

"I'm not happy about it and it will take a while until I can trust you again. But I don't want it to happen a second time. Is that clear ?"

"Yes Sir," I said loud and clear.

"You called me Sir. That always makes me horny," Colton said.

"Good to know Sir. From now on I will call you Sir five times a day Sir. Or more."

"It won't help you tonight though. You're still grounded and I don't do sloppy seconds anyway. I bet his cum is still in your ass. If I stick my dick in there it probably will run out. That actually sounds hot, damn it. Now I'm horny," Colton admitted and rearranged his dick and balls.

He told me to drop my pants and to bend over. He said he wants to examine my man cave. He didn't have to tell me twice. I was naked in no time and bent over to give him free easy access to my man cave, as he called it. He probed me with one finger. No cum came out. He stretched my hole open with his left and right middle finger. Still nothing. "No cum in there babe. Did you absorb it or what did your hungry ass do with it ? Maybe that loser Jan shoots blanks," Colton laughed.

"I don't know, maybe his 10 incher pushed it deep, very deep down my fuckhole. But I wouldn't call him a loser. He is just a man with needs who is looking for love and fell for me as you did one year ago babe," I said to Colton.

"You're right. It's just jealousy that makes me talk like this," he responded.

He pulled his fingers out of me and my hole tightened up again.

"Alright than, no sex for me tonight," I repeated Colton's words.

Jan didn't call or text at all. I was still thinking about him and hoping he was alright. About three month had passed since I saw him the last time. By then he was probably over me I figured. I don't know why I got the idea and went to his office one day. Just to see he was ok I guess. I asked his secretary if he was in his office. She told me he is in a meeting. I asked her how he is doing as far as she knows. "He seems kinda depressed lately, that's all I can say," she said. I thanked her for the info and left the office. I walked slowly to my car and had a cigarette. I hoped Jan was doing better but if he seemed depressed and his secretary even noticed it, then he wasn't doing alright at all. I was still sitting in my car and finished the cigarette, when I saw Jan's car. He parked not far from me. I didn't know if I should talk to him or if it's better to leave him alone. But it was too late. He got out of his car and walked towards the office building, when he suddenly stopped. He saw my car and we looked directly in each other's eyes. I got out of the car and stood only ten feet away from him. I think we both had the same thoughts. Should we engage in a conversation or just walk away. I wanted to leave it up to him but I started talking to him anyway.

"How are you doing Jan ? I didn't know if I should come to your office or not. But I was thinking about you and I felt guilty about not even asking if you're ok."

"I'm doing fine. Don't worry about me. I work hard, make good money and go back and forth to my house in Brazil," he answered.

"That's all ? Working and going to Brazil ? No dating ?" I asked him.

"Dating ? Are you kidding me ? I told you before I don't want anybody else. I want you. Even if I find someone I love, in the back of my mind there will always be you, the man I really want," he said.

Damn, he really fell bad for me. I didn't know it was that intense.

"I'm very sorry Jan, I wish I could solve that problem. If you want I can come over to your house and we talk if it makes you feel better. Oh god, I'm talking bull crap.

How can it make you feel better? You know what I mean. But if you want, let me know and I'll stop by."

"Ok, I will see. I got to go," he said and walked away. He turned around one more time though and looked at me with his sad puppy eyes. I drove back home thinking about Jan. I couldn't go home. I turned around and went back to Jan's office. Before I went inside I called Colton.

"Hey babe. Just wanted to say I love you and I'm home shortly."

"Ok baby boy see ya in a bit. Love you too."

I wasn't sure anymore if I should go back inside. I took off again. Half way home I pulled over. I tried not to cry but I was very close. Did I fall for Jan and didn't even know ? But I loved Colton and would never do anything to hurt him. I turned around again and parked at

Jan's office. I walked inside through his secretary's office and asked her if Jan was by himself. She said yes but he had told her to cancel all his appointments and he doesn't wanna be bothered.

I told her it's ok and he wouldn't mind seeing me.

"Oh are you the young man he fell in love with and is always talking about ?" she asked me.

"He told you ?" I said.

"Yes, only a few times. He has nobody else to talk to," she said.

That made me even feel worse. I opened the door to his office and went inside.

Jan was sitting at his desk, his back turned towards the door.

"Didn't I say I don't wanna be bothered Ms. Turner ?" he said. I got closer to him and put my hand on his shoulder without saying anything.

He turned his head. When he saw me I noticed his cute puppy eyes started to look brighter, almost sparkling.

"I had to come back. I can't stand seeing you like this. I'm always there for you if you need me, I want you to remember that," I said and walked towards the door.

"Please don't go," he said and got off the chair. We walked towards each other. When I was standing in front of him he hugged me tight and was in tears.

"I don't know what to do. I don't wanna live without you. I know it sounds selfish," he said.

I thought about a way to make him feel better. I gave him a kiss and told him: "I'm gonna see you tomorrow, ok ? We spend some time together at your house and you get to know me better. Maybe you don't even want me anymore, when you find out what an ass I am. I laughed and he smiled at me.

"That sounds nice, I like the idea. But what about you ? I don't want you to get in trouble because of me. I'm glad you stopped by. It was a nice surprise. I can make us something to eat and a few drinks or we can BBQ at the pool," he said and put his head on my shoulder.

"Ok sounds great," I answered. He gave me another kiss before I left his office. I had to hurry to get back home. Colton was waiting to have dinner with me.

I went to the kitchen. Colton was standing at the stove and made gravy for the mashed potatoes. He gave me a kiss and smacked my butt.

"Where have you been all afternoon," Colton asked me.

"I had to run a few errands," I said. I felt like such a lying slut. Colton is too good to me and I don't deserve him. But on the other hand it's not my fault that two guys fell in love with me, I tried to justify my behavior.

Dinner was ready. Colton made meatloaf, mashed potatoes and gravy.

"Come on you spoiled brat, dinner is ready," he called." We ate in the kitchen but I wasn't really hungry. I had to stop what was between Jan and me. I decided to go to his house the next day as I promised Jan but that's it. I would be there for him if he needs me but nothing else.

"You seem kinda preoccupied tonight, what's the matter baby boy ?" Colton asked.

"Oh nothing really, just tired. I like when you call me your baby boy. Wanna go early to bed and cuddle and go from there ?"

"Sure why not," Colton answered.

We cleaned up the kitchen together and hit the hay. I put my arm around Colton's waist. My hand rested on his balls and dick. But I was too distracted to concentrate on making love to Colton. Colton was asleep already anyway so I didn't feel too bad about it.

The next day was a Sunday. For a few weeks Colton went every Sunday from 11am to 1pm to a nearby church. The service and a social gathering afterwards took about two hours. He left the house around 10.30am. It made it easier for me. I didn't have to come up with a lie.

I left the house five minutes after Colton. I had about three hours I could spend with Jan. It took me only twenty minutes to get to his house. He came outside when he saw me parking in his driveway and opened the car door for me.

"Hey my handsome gentleman," I said. He smiled at me and gave me a kiss. He was hiding something in his left hand behind his back. When I got out of my car he gave me a bouquet of edible red roses.

"Oh my god, Jan. They are beautiful and look so real. Thank you so much."

"You are very welcome. You don't know how much you coming over today means to me. Come inside. I made Chicken Cordon bleu for us. I hope you like it," Jan told me. He seemed really happy.

"I would like anything you cooked. Cordon bleu is Colton's favorite dish but I like it too." I didn't even finish my last sentence when Jan lost the smile on his face.

"Oh I'm sorry Jan. It just came out. I didn't mean to remind you, well you know about what."

"I know, that's ok. Don't worry babe," Jan responded.

He already called me babe. I was afraid he thought there was more between him and me then there really was. I thought I was clear enough about it.

"Oh, you babe me ?" I asked him.

"Does it bother you ? I won't if you don't like it," he said.

"It doesn't bother me. It's just that Colton calls me babe."

"Oh I see. How stupid of me. I should've known. Ok I won't say it again. Let's have a drink for our friendship," Jan said.

"Yeah that sounds good to me. I emptied my glass in three seconds. I took one edible red rose and was holding it close to his mouth. He bit a big piece off it. He came closer to me and kissed me with the rose still in his mouth. I could taste the sweet flavor of the sugar. He stopped kissing and just looked at me. He took the rose stem out of my hand and fed it to me. When I got to the end of the stem, he fed me his finger.

I sucked on it like it was his dick. My cock was already getting bigger. I had to stop. I promised Colton it would never happen again. On the other hand he fell asleep on me and deprived me of my sexual activity. I knew I was just looking for an excuse to fuck with Jan. And this one was a stupid excuse.

"Jan, you make me horny. I mean I was horny already but you turned me on. Remember when we said it can't happen again ?"

"Yes, I remember. I got carried away. Sorry. But I'm crazy about you. Everything about you turns me on. Your smile, your voice, your eyes, the way you talk and your gestures, everything," Jan said to me.

"Same here if I'm honest. But I'm also crazy about Colton. I should've left you alone like you told me to. Now we made it even worse. But it's easier to say than actually doing it," I said.

"I know. Let's enjoy the time we have together today and see how we feel and think about it tomorrow," Jan said.

We were sitting at the pool and had lunch. I had another drink and forgot all about my alcohol abstinence. When I had my third drink I remembered but it was too late. I told Jan about the alcohol problem I had. He felt terrible that he offered me alcohol, but he didn't know. As always when I got drunk, I was thinking with my dick head. I forgot the time limit I had to be home before Colton was back from church. I opened Jans zipper and put my hand inside his pants. I pulled his dick out and was about to suck him off when he stopped me.

"No Kent, you're drunk. I can't take advantage of that. Tomorrow you would hate me if I let you suck me off. How do you get home on time anyway ? You can't drive like that. What are you gonna tell Colton ?" Jan asked me.

I didn't care. I was feeling good and I was with Jan. Anything else didn't count at that time.

Jan put me in the passenger seat and drove my car close to Colton's house. About a quarter mile before we got to the house, Jan stopped and told me to drive home myself. I couldn't do much wrong driving only a quarter mile. But either way Colton would notice that I'm drunk. I could see Jan felt guilty about the alcohol incident but it wasn't his fault. He gave me a kiss goodbye and took a cab back home.

Colton was already home. I didn't know what to tell him why I was drunk. I parked the car in the garage and stumbled inside the house.

"Where have you been babe ? I tried to call you," Colton asked me.

"Aw, hold on. I have to go to the bathroom first," I answered. I thought if I puke, the alcohol effect wouldn't last as long. I stuck one finger in my throat and threw up.

I went back to the living room where Colton was watching Tv.

"Hey baby girl, how was church ?" I asked.

"As always, it was nice. Do you feel alright ? You look like you're drunk. Where have you been ?"

I remembered Colton's words: Honesty is always the best. "Aw, well I was driving around," I said.

"Yeah I could've guessed that," Colton answered.

"And then I forgot I'm not supposed to drink alcohol. But I did. I did it three times babe. Imagine I had three drinks baby."

That was the moment when I fell off the couch.

Colton dragged me back on it. I heard him saying "drunk pig" at some point. When I woke up again I yelled:

"Babe where are you ? I need to tell you something."

"I'm right here. Why are you yelling ?"

"Oh sorry. I need to tell you something. Something important. Yeah I have to tell you, I had a few drinks," I mumbled.

"No.Really ? I wouldn't have known if you hadn't told me baby," Colton answered and laughed.

"But you promised me you won't touch alcohol again. So why did you break your own rule ? What made you drink again ? You know you get your butt kicked or spanked for that," Colton said.

"Yes. Spanking is good. I like spanking my monkey," I said to Colton, still drunk as shit.

"Oh no. I'm not talking about spanking your monkey. I'm talking about whipping your ass if you understand that better.

I woke up, still laying on the couch, around 1pm on the next day. I suddenly remembered that I was drinking. I jumped off the couch and looked for Colton. I was afraid I did some crazy shit when I was drunk. I probably fucked it up with Jan too.

Colton was outside cutting grass. I took my phone to call Jan. On my call log were three calls from him. When I called back I apologized for whatever I had done, when I was drunk. He told me I didn't do anything crazy last night, he just called to see if I was alright. I told him I just woke up and I was doing ok. I told Jan I would call him back later, after I talked to Colton.

I went outside to Colton. He just got done cutting the lawn. I told him I had a few drinks because I felt guilty about Jan.

"Jan. Guilty. Why ? Is he still bothering you ?" Colton asked.

I told Colton I ran into Jan's secretary the other day and she had told me about Jan being depressed and all that. Colton didn't ask or say much more about it. I called Jan later at night.

"Hey Jan. Everything is ok. Thanks for the nice time with you. I enjoyed it," I told him.

"Yeah I know. You enjoyed it a little too much," he said and laughed.

We started calling each other every day from that moment on. Every Sunday, when Colton went to church, I saw Jan at his place. We didn't have sex, just hanging out. But I had a bad conscience about the whole situation and I got more and more depressed. I couldn't tell Colton that I was hanging out with Jan for a few weeks.

One evening though, I had to tell him.

It was when Jan called me.I left my phone in the bedroom, when I had to go to the bathroom and take a piss. Colton answered my phone because usually only mutual friends of ours or my parents would call my phone and we had no secrets from each other. Well, except the one.

Jan didn't recognize Colton's voice right away.

"Hey Kenty boy. I had a good time today. Just wanna say thanks and good night," Jan said.

"Who is this ?" Colton asked. "And why did you have a good time with 'Kenty boy' ?"

That was the moment when Jan realized what he just did. He hung up without saying anything.

"Kent ! Can you come back for a moment please ? It won't take long, I can promise you that."

"Hold on. I have to dry my dick off first or I will get piss stains all over my pants."

I went back to the bedroom and laid down on the bed next to Colton.

"You just got a call 'Kenty boy,'" was all Colton said. I knew who called, he didn't have to tell me.

"Oh yeah. I wanted to tell you something babe. I just didn't know how. I was afraid you would get angry," I answered.

"Did you. Well, I'm listening. That was Jan Sorensen, wasn't it ?" Colton said a little upset.

"I felt so bad because I couldn't give Jan what he was looking for. He said he doesn't wanna meet any other guys. If he can't have me he would rather stay single," I explained.

"Oh and you had to come to the rescue and play mother Theresa to comfort him of course," Colton said.

"Yes. I mean no. I just thought if I hang out with him it makes him feel better."

"Just hanging out huh ? You're such a Saint Kent."

"I promise babe I did not have sex with him. Just hanging out for a couple hours," I said.

To my surprise Colton stayed pretty much calm.

"So do I have to be afraid of you leaving me for him ?" Colton asked.

"Hell no. I told you I can't be without you and I meant it," I said.

"Ok. I believe you. But you have to stop seeing him. I'm not sharing you with your lover boy. You have to decide between me or him. This is my last word about it," Colton said.

I felt so shitty. Jan knew I wouldn't break up with Colton and Colton knew I had some feelings for Jan.

"Colton, I can't tell Jan I can't see him any more. I can't look into his eyes and say goodbye. I'm not strong enough."

"I know it's not easy but I can prime him for you if you want. I talk to him first. I call him right now," Colton said and took the phone to call Jan. I went outside when he talked to him.

"Hey Jan, it's Colton. I asked Kent what was going on and he told me. I can totally understand your feelings for Kent but you wouldn't like it either if he is your husband and seeing someone else on the side. I told Kent he can't continue seeing you. I think you understand. Kent is gonna call you to tell you himself. He just has a hard time telling you so he went outside."

Jan started crying on the phone and hung up.

"Kent, you can come back inside."

"How did it go ?" I asked when I came back inside.

"He cried and hung up after I told him. I feel for the guy but he wouldn't care about me when he could take you away from me," Colton said. I didn't wanna talk to Jan when Colton was around. It was awkward. I texted him instead.

"Jan, you know I love you. But I have no other choice.I can't see you anymore. I stop by tomorrow and we talk.

Love you

Kent"

I stopped by Jan's office the next day. His secretary told me he didn't come in that morning. I drove to his house and went inside. He gave me a key to his front door a few weeks ago. He was lying on his bed and sleeping. It smelled like alcohol in the bedroom. I found an empty bottle of Rum on the floor.

"Damn Jan, you really did a good job this time, didn't you," I said to myself. I was shaking him to wake him up. He slowly opened his eyes. He smiled when he recognized me.

"You really came over today, I thought I would never see you again," he said.

"Of course. I told you I would," I said and tried to pull him off the bed.

"Come on you heavy Sea Cow. You have to take a shower. You smell like alcohol and sweat."

He got up and was already naked. His dick was semi hard. I guided him to the shower and turned the cold water on to sober him up. His dick turned from half hard to totally soft in seconds. I laughed and said: "Are you awake now ? I will take care of your dick later, don't worry. I get it hard again." I dried him off with an oversized towel. I gave him a hug and a kiss. We went to the living room and were sitting on the couch, when Colton called: "Where are you babe ? Everything ok ?"

I told him: "Yes but I called Jan to talk to him and couldn't get a hold of him. His secretary told me he didn't show up at the office. Now I'm driving around to find him. I hope he is ok."

"I hope so too. Anyway, I have a surprise for you when you get back. I thought it would cheer you up after the thing with Jan," Colton said.

"Thanks babe. See ya soon," I said and hung up.

Jan and I made out on the couch. We kissed and cuddled and enjoyed each other. About one hour later Jan got quiet and seemed depressed again.

"Kent, I had a good time with you today. But this has to be the last time we hang out together. We can't be just friends. We keep hurting ourselves and others if we continue this. You made your decision to stay with Colton. Maybe someday if the time is right and if something should happen between you and Colton we could be together," Jan said. We both were in tears.

"I know. If I would leave Colton for you I wouldn't be happy either and would wanna see and hang out with him. I don't know what's wrong with me. I want you to call me babe one more time babe," I said to Jan. He kissed me and said: I love you babe. I will never forget you and you will always have a place in my heart. You be careful and take good care of yourself babe. Every night at 10pm I will look up to the sky. I will look at the big, bright star to the left and I will think about you. If you do the same, we can be together in our thoughts every night.'`

"That's a wonderful and sweet idea. I will look at our star every night, I promise," I said to Jan.

I almost cried when I left. On my way home I stopped at the beach. I was the only person there. I just stood there and looked at the endless ocean.

At the same time Jan was standing at his bedroom window and looking at the Lake next to his property.

The song 'Try' came to my mind where it says 'Why do we fall in love so easily even when it's not right' and 'Where there is desire there is gonna be a flame, where there is a flame someone's bound to get burned.'

It's so true. I continued my way home to Colton.

I was curious what surprise he had for me. When I drove through the gate I saw Colton's Dad's old Rolls Royce parked outside the garage with a new license plate. Colton must've registered it and put a big red bow on top of the hood.

I went inside the house and found Colton in the bathroom taking a shower.

"Hey Mister naked man. Need a shower ? What's up with the Rolls ?" I asked.

"I got it registered today and had it in the shop for inspection. It's ready for you whenever you want," Colton told me.

"You're a crazy fucker Colton," I laughed. "Thank you. That was a nice idea. I'll take it for a spin right now," I said. I took the keys and went outside again. It was the first time I was sitting or driving in a Rolls. It was dark blue on the outside and had cream colored leather seats. I drove to Jan's house but I didn't stop or go inside. His car was parked in the driveway. I turned around and drove back home."Drives beautiful," I said to Colton.

"Yeah. It's been a long time since I drove it the last time. I never registered it because it's too fancy for me. I love my Corvette. But I kept it because it was Dad's baby," Colton told me.

I wanted to show Jan the Rolls and take him for a ride, but I thought one goodbye was enough in one day for him and me.

10 pm came closer and I got ready to look at Jan's and my star. I walked to the pool where it was dark and Colton wasn't around. At ten o'clock sharp I looked up to the sky. There was the big bright star Jan was looking at, right at that moment. "You have a good night Jan," I said to myself, while looking at the star.

The next day I took the Rolls to run a few errands. The good thing was nobody would recognize me in it. I stopped across the street from Jan's office. I just sat in the car and waited until Jan would show up. I wanted to see him only for the few seconds it took him to walk from his car to the building. But he didn't show up. I drove to his house. His car was still parked in the driveway. It didn't take me longer than two hours to do all my errands. Before I went home I drove by Jan's house again. His car was there.

10pm that night I looked at our star and wished Jan a good night again. I dialed his number and let the phone ring twice before I hung up. He also let my phone ring and we both knew the other one was ok.

"What are you doing out there in the dark ?" Colton asked me and I wished I could've told him the truth. "I was just looking at the stars," I said, which wasn't really a lie. I was hungry for some ice cream. I remembered we still had some in the freezer. I made a bowl for me and Colton. We went outside to the pool and enjoyed our ice cream under a clear sky on a full moon night.

"We have a full moon babe. Look how big it is. My Dad used to say crazy things happen during a full moon night," Colton said.

"Yeah maybe. When I was younger I usually couldn't sleep, when we had a full moon. Oh, the Owl must be back, did you hear it ?" I asked.

"Yes I heard it. I don't really care about Owls. They are creepy birds. I always get goosebumps when I hear them. My Dad also used to say somebody is dying, when you hear an Owl hooting," Colton told me.

"I believe that's superstitious stuff," I said.

I was thinking about Jan, what he was doing at the moment. I decided to spy on him again in the morning, when he goes to work. Suddenly I had the perfect idea for a role play. I had to text it to Jan.

"Hey Jan, I know I'm not supposed to contact you but I have to tell you this. How about I need a lawyer and come to your office. You sit at your desk in a dress shirt and tie but your pants hanging around your ankles. I'm about to knock at your door but it's not closed all the way. I can see you sitting there and playing with your cock. You see me spy on you and you come to the door, drag me in and fuck the shit out of me right there in front of your male secretary. Lol.

Just came to my mind and I thought I would share it with you. Good night. Love ya always

Kent"

It was already midnight, so I didn't expect him to text back. Colton and I went to bed shortly after I texted.

I got up early the next morning to make sure I'm at Jan's office before he gets there. I parked across the street again and waited for him to show up. But he didn't come to the office again. After I waited for two hours I gave up. I drove to his house and his car was still parked at the same spot in his driveway as the day before. He probably was drinking again to get me off his mind. That was the third day he didn't go to work because he was drunk.

I texted him to see if he was ok or needed anything but he didn't respond. I gave him the key to his house back the day before, otherwise I would've gone inside. I drove to his office again and asked his secretary Ms. Fink if she knew anything. She told me Jan called her yesterday afternoon and said he would be back to work today and if not he would give her a call. She asked me: "Why don't you go and check on him. I thought you both live together as boyfriends ?"

"No we don't. And we're not exactly boyfriends but that's a different story," I said to her.

"Ah, ok. He always referred to you as his boyfriend, that's why I asked," she said.

I gave her my phone number so she could call me if she knows anything new about Jan.

From Jan's office I drove straight home.

"Oh hey you're back. You like riding in the Rolls, don't ya," Colton asked.

"Yeah I do. It's different but if you drive it around here just to go to the store or so, it feels like when you go to a BBQ in a suit and tie," I said.

I didn't hear anything from Jan or Ms. Fink that afternoon. I waited until 10pm and let Jans phone ring twice again when I looked at our star. But he didn't ring back. I was getting worried and did not get much sleep that night. I wished I could tell Colton about it but that was no option.

At 9am I was back at Jan's office but he didn't show up for work again. I finally called his phone but the call went straight to his voicemail box. I had to go over to his house and check on him. I felt bad that I didn't do it already the day before.

He didn't answer the door when I got there and knocked. I felt fear creeping up my spine. Fear that something could've happened to him. I left his house, there was no way to get inside, except climbing over the fence. If I wouldn't hear from him by late afternoon, I would call the cops.

I was halfway home, when I decided to turn around and climb over Jans fence. And I told Colton about it. I called him and said Ms. Fink, Jans secretary, called and asked me if I knew where Jan was. He didn't show up at the office the past three days. Colton actually encouraged me to go and check on him.

I parked in his driveway, jumped out of my car and ran to the fence in Jan's backyard. I saw a neighbor and called him over to help me climb over the fence. He lifted me up and when I was on top of it, I saw Jan floating in his pool. I thought it was great, everybody is worried and he is relaxing in the pool. But he wasn't moving. I jumped off the fence and ran as fast as I could to Jan. I pulled him out of the pool and yelled to the neighbor to call 911. I did CPR but he didn't start breathing on his own. I kept breathing in his mouth until the ambulance arrived.

"That was a good thing to do. You probably saved his life by doing CPR. How did it happen ?" the doctor asked me.

"I don't know. I wasn't here. I just checked on him cuz he didn't go to his office the past three days. I guess he was drunk and fell in the pool or something. It must've happened not too long ago. If I had waited until the afternoon as I was planning, it would've been too late," I told the doctor.

They flew him in a helicopter to the nearest hospital. He was in the ICU when I got there. The doctor told me it seemed like he was at least ten minutes without oxygen. That means he could have permanent brain damage. Since he had no relatives, they probably would release him to a mental institute.

I was devastated. He was on life support, nobody knew for how long. When I came home Colton saw on my face that something was wrong. "What happened ? Everything ok, did you find him ?" he asked.

I told him what happened.

"That's terrible. I'm glad you got there on time and could save his life," Colton said.

"Yeah. He could be dead now. He has no relatives and if he wakes up and can breathe on his own again, the hospital is gonna release him to a mental institution," I told Colton.

"Oh, I'm sorry to hear that. Why ? Is he gonna be, well you know what I mean," Colton said.

"It's a 90% possibility, yes."

"Poor guy. He shouldn't drink so much," was all Colton had to say.

"Oh shit, I forgot to call Jans secretary. She doesn't even know yet," I said. I told Colton I would visit Jan every day. He didn't say anything against it but I knew he wasn't crazy about it either. I called Ms. Fink and told her everything that happened.

She started crying. I said: "The doctors don't know if or when Jan comes out of the coma. I guess you have to look for another job. I don't know what's gonna happen with all his stuff and the business."

She said: "I know that Jan has a last Will. He just changed it a few weeks ago. He also signed a power of attorney. It's all in the office safe over here in a sealed envelope. I'm gonna open it and see what's in it." She hung up but wanted to call me back shortly. I went to the bathroom and took a piss. I started to feel nauseous. Colton came in and said: "Looks like I'm coming at the right time. But you need to wash your dick babe. I need to piss too."

Ms. Fink called me ten minutes later about Jan's last Will.

"Kent, you won't believe this. His last Will is in your name. You get everything he owns and I get ten grand. I mean if he would pass away. He also gave you power of attorney in case something like this would happen."

"Oh. He did ?" I said. I was kinda speechless for a few seconds. I told her I was going to see her the next morning in the office.

When I told Colton about the Will he acted kinda strange.

"Well then you don't need me anymore I guess, if you get all his money. Why would he give you everything ?"

"Babe. First at all I'm not with you because of your money and second, I guess because Jan has no relatives. And as you know he likes me so that's why he wants me to have it. But he's not dead. I just have to make the decisions for him now," I said to Colton.

The next morning I went over to Jan's office to meet Ms. Fink. We were reading the Will and power of attorney together.

One part in his Will said:

I want Kent Sabel to have my house in Brazil, the house in Miami and all other assets including the cash in all my bank accounts. I want Kent to give Ms. Fink a one time payment of $ 10,000.

Now everything was so real.

I had to cancel the lease for the office first. Later down the road I probably would sell the house in Brazil, depending on Jan's condition. I went to Jan's house and cleaned up the bedroom and living room. There were empty bottles laying around on the floor everywhere. In the bedroom he puked on the carpet. But I got everything cleaned up after about one hour. Then I had to do the hard part, visiting Jan in the hospital. I didn't wanna see him like that, connected to wires and tubes.

I got to Jan's room in the ICU around noon. There has been no change since the day before. He was still connected to the breathing tube. I took his hand and held it for the entire time I was there. I also talked to him. I was sure he could hear me. I still think Colton heard me talking to him and it helped him to come out of his coma.

"Jan it's me, Kent. Don't worry, everything will be ok. I will always be there for you. I will see you every day and I will annoy the shit out of you until you wake up. I do love you Jan, you know that right ?" I said to him in a calm tone. His hand was slightly squeezing mine, I wasn't sure. It could've been a muscle spasm or something. Then I thought I saw him opening his left eye and closing it. I told the nurse about it. I had to go home so I wouldn't piss off Colton.

"I have to leave for a while but I will be back soon baby. Yes, I called you baby. You heard right. And when I come back I want you to tell me what happened. Ok ? Love you."

I left and drove straight home. I told Colton about my day and Jan.

"Don't you wanna visit Jan too ?" I asked Colton but I should've known the answer.

"Maybe," was all he said.

"Colton, I'm gonna take care of Jan if he needs it. I can't let him rot in a mental place for the rest of his life."

"I figured you would. But how is this gonna be ? You need to move into his house or he has to stay here ?"

"I was thinking he stays here if that's ok with you. I can't move in there and you live here," I explained to Colton.

After only three days, Jan came out of his coma. A nurse from the hospital called me at 7pm and told me Jan is awake. I told Colton that Jan woke up and I needed to go to see him.

When I got to the hospital Jan wasn't in the ICU anymore. He was sitting up in his bed and smiled when he recognized me.

"Hey Jan, I'm so glad to see you up and kicking."

He still looked at me and smiled. The nurse waved at me from the door. I followed her outside the room. Jans doctor was there too and wanted to talk to me.

"Hi, I'm Patricia. Jan Sorensen's Doctor. I want to give you a heads up about your friend. Because of the extended time of being without oxygen, Jan suffers from loss of many brain cells. The body will regenerate most of those cells but not all and it will take time. He recognized you, which is a good sign. So far he hasn't spoken since he woke up. It may take therapy and rehab to teach him to speak, maybe he starts talking on his own again. It's complicated to say with brain injuries. It's possible that he has to learn certain other things too like using the bathroom or reading and writing. We wanna keep him a few more days in here before we admit him to a different facility."

"You mean a looney bin, right ?" I said.

"I wouldn't call it that, it's a rehab center for mentally challenged people, where he gets the best care 24/7" the doctor told me.

"And where he is around less fortunate people than him. And if they get too much of a nuisance they get medication that keeps them calm and looney. I take him home and care for him. I go with him to his therapy every day," I told her and made it very clear what I want.

She still kept trying to talk me into the mental rehab place until I snapped. I wished Colton would've been there to talk to her. Even after my counseling I still got upset easily.

"Didn't you hear what I just said ? Are you a natural blonde ? You're probably affiliated with that place. You're all money hungry bastards. You don't really care what happens to Jan," I yelled at her. She thought she had to show her authority to me and started talking louder: "Mr. Sabel, this is going too far. You are leaving this hospital right now and I make sure you won't enter it ever again."

"Well, make me leave. You can lick my ass." It made her even more upset and I enjoyed it. I called Colton right in front of her and told him to come over as soon as possible.

"Colton, I need you here at the hospital as my lawyer right now."

"What did you do again ? Why do you need me there ? Oh I know why. You need me to talk to someone because your big mouth got you in trouble, right ?"

"Yep. Right," I answered Colton.

"My lawyer is on his way and we're gonna sue your ass," I said to the doctor.

I went back to Jan until Colton arrived.

Jan was smiling again but didn't talk. At least she was right about one thing, I thought.

"Jan, can you understand me ? Do you know who I am ?" He kept smiling. I started to freak out. Was this all what was left from Jan ? All he could do was smile ?

"Jan, do you know me ?"

Suddenly he nodded his head. He touched my cheek with his right hand. I kissed his hand and asked if he wanted some paper and a pen to write something down. He shook his head but I gave him a pen and paper anyway to see what he was gonna do. It must be frightening if you wake up in a hospital and don't know why. And you can't even ask somebody because you notice you can't talk or write something down. He held the pen in his hand and looked at it. He started drawing on the paper. I thought he didn't forget how to write and he's writing down a question. But he was just drawing something that looked like a full moon and a lake.

I heard Colton talking to the doctor. He just arrived. He apologized in my name and sweet talked to her. I guess it helped because she didn't pursue me, me getting kicked out of the hospital.

Colton came into the room to see Jan, since he was there anyway. He was shocked when he saw Jan.

"Jan, if you understand me, nod your head please," I said again. He nodded. That helps a lot when he understands what I'm saying. I told him what happened and why he is in the hospital. I also told him he's gonna live with Colton and me until he gets better. I didn't tell him he may not get better at all.

"Ok my handsome man, I have to go home now. I will see you tomorrow. I will take you home soon." I was wondering if he still knew what being gay means and that he is a gay man. Or if he remembers sex and what you can do with your dick. I could teach him that easily if I needed to, I thought.

Colton and I left the hospital to go home and relax. But my mind couldn't relax. I was thinking about Jan and his condition.

"By the way Colton, thanks for rescuing my ass from that vicious doctor today. And thanks for letting Jan stay here," I said.

"No problem. I didn't think I would ever see Jan like that. It's so sad. We will take good care of him. We owe him that," Colton answered.

"Yeah. And I never thought we would live in a polyamorous relationship with Jan," I said.

"I wouldn't call it polyamorous because we don't have a romantic relationship with him, right ?"

"Aw yeah right," I mumbled.

Jan had to stay five more days in the hospital. They already had started the therapy. I picked him up at 10am on a Friday morning. I took him by his arm and guided him to the car. I drove with him to his house first. I wanted to see if he remembers his home or not. Especially the pool. When we got there he looked at the house for a few seconds. That was all he did. "Come on Jan get out the car. We went inside the house for a bit. It's your house, remember ?" I gave him his keys but he just played with them in his hand. We got out of the car and walked towards the front door. I showed him how to unlock and open the door. We walked through the house and to the pool in the backyard. When he saw the pool it seemed like something clicked. He looked around and acted nervous. I told him that I found him in his pool at the last second. He hugged me tight so he must've understood me.

We left his house and went to Colton's place. He was around me all day and I showed him everything. To get food from the fridge, taking a shower, taking a piss or shit. And he learned quickly to a certain extent. I was curious if he remembered sex though. One Sunday morning, when Colton went to church again I got naked and laid next to Jan on his bed. I played with my dick and it got hard. Jan was watching me but didn't do anything. I told him to pull his pants down. He took his pants and t-shirt off. I grabbed his cock and stroked him slowly. I told him to do the same with my cock. He did for a while but stopped, when I took his dick in my mouth and sucked on it. He was moaning and grabbing his balls. His dick started to get hard. I kept sucking until I tasted his precum. So far everything is working down there, I thought. But then he got soft again. I didn't care and continued sucking his head. Suddenly his body was shaking and I got scared. I thought I may have overstimulated him and he's getting a seizure or something. But I was wrong. He pumped a huge cum load up to his piss slit from where it sprayed into my mouth and down my throat.

"Wow, thanks Jan. Did you like it ? Do you remember when we fucked around in your office one time ?" I asked him. He nodded twice. "Well, you learned another thing today. I'm glad I could teach and show you. You probably will do it every day again from now on," I said. He nodded again and smiled.

Colton also showed him things around the house and yard. Jan started talking again after about three month. Not like he did before though. He talked slower and pronounced some words differently. He also was forgetful. It didn't get better and he never learned reading, writing or driving a car again. But otherwise he recuperated very well. I also didn't have to remind him again to jerk off together on Sundays. After about one year we sold his house but kept the one in Brazil, where everything began. We are best friends now and he lives in one part of the house. Colton and I do everything for him that he can't do on his own. Colton is not jealous anymore. He knows Jan loves me and I love Jan but it actually strengthened our love and marriage. Now we know nothing can break us apart.

www.ingramcontent.com/pod-product-compliance
Lightning Source LLC
Chambersburg PA
CBHW050539160726
48003CB00002B/664